**Also available from
Chantal Fernando**

The Knights & Dragons MC Series

Decker's Dilemma
Rhett Redeemed

The Fast & Fury Series

Custom Built
Custom Made
Custom Love

The Knights of Fury
MC Series

Saint
Renegade
Temper

The Wind Dragons
MC Series

Dragon's Lair
Arrow's Hell
Tracker's End
Dirty Ride
Rake's Redemption
Wild Ride
Wolf's Mate
Last Ride
Crossroads

**The Cursed Ravens
MC Series**

*Ace of Hearts
Knuckle Down
Going Rogue*

The Conflict of Interest Series

*Breaching the Contract
Seducing the Defendant
Approaching the Bench
Leading the Witness*

LOVE
GRUDGE

CHANTAL FERNANDO

carina
press

carina
press®

Recycling programs
for this product may
not exist in your area.

ISBN-13: 978-1-335-47541-1

Love Grudge

For questions and comments about the quality of this book,
please contact us at CustomerService@Harlequin.com.

Carina Press
22 Adelaide St. West, 41st Floor
Toronto, Ontario M5H 4E3, Canada
www.CarinaPress.com

Printed in U.S.A.

For Ty,

Congrats on winning your first fight.

I've never been more proud, and scared, in my life.

And just because you see me on TikTok
every time you walk into my room
doesn't mean I'm not working.

If my laptop is open, I'm on the clock.

Love you, my baby boy.

"My only love sprung from my only hate
Too early seen unknown, and known too late!"
—William Shakespeare, *Romeo & Juliet*

Chapter One

Romeo

Fingers tapping on the steering wheel to the sound of Tupac, I wait for Rosalind to get into my car so she and I can have a chat.

This "chat" has been a long time coming—our on-again, off-again secret romance needs to come to an end. It was fun while it lasted, but now reality has come for me. When we met, it was supposed to be a one-time thing. But one time turned into two, two into three. And now I find myself here two months later in a quasi-relationship with a woman I can never really be with. But as much fun as I had with her, I knew it was just that and we were not meant to ride into the sunset together.

The timing couldn't be better. I'm not sure what other stories you've been told about motorcycle clubs, or MCs as popular culture tends to refer to them, but my club operates a bit like a monarchy. My father is the president of the Devils MC and my grandfather was president before him. But unlike a monarchy, the president does not keep the role until their death, only until they turn fifty. So as per tradition in my family, with my father's upcoming birthday, *I* am going to become president of the Devils MC.

Becoming president is a gig I've been born into, and something I've been getting ready for my entire life. But now that it's here, I don't feel like I thought I would. This moment has been hyped up for my entire life, and now it's a little anticlimactic. All I'm about to inherit is a whole lot of responsibility.

And power.

Power is good, but it comes with a price. And Rosalind is the first casualty.

The lithe blonde with a killer body opens the car door and slides in, her rose scent hitting me before her brown eyes do. When she turns to me, her eyes are flat and a little red from crying.

"What's wrong?" I ask, instantly going on alert. "Are you okay?" I'm not a monster. Just because she isn't the love of my life doesn't mean I don't give a shit.

"My grandfather died this morning," she says, wrapping her arms around herself. Her long blonde hair drapes her face like a curtain, some of the strands stuck to her cheek from the tears. I stare straight ahead, processing this information.

Mikey Callisto is dead. The OG biker from the Angels MC.

An MC that was formed due to their history with my family.

I forgot to mention that part.

The Devils are destined to hate the Angels. We are not to intermingle, not to have anything to do with one another. The history is quite simple—it was over a girl. My grandfather was in love with a woman called Libby Rose and he was going to marry her. Until she fell in love with my grandfather's best friend, Mikey Callisto. In an effort to maintain peace, my grandfather's father, then president of the Devils MC, allowed Mikey and Libby Rose to leave the MC and start a new one so long as their operations did not conflict with Devils MC business. In exchange, Mikey agreed to give the Devils MC twenty percent of all income for forty-five years, which coincidentally ends in a month. We've had a semblance of a truce ever since, but with the ending of the debt tax, I have no idea what I'll be inheriting. I'm just waiting for something to happen.

Rosalind glances over at me, and I wince. I guess I haven't completely left the Angels alone.

But the weird thing is, I've been told all my life that the Angels were the enemies. Except I've never seen it that way. They did their thing, we did ours. We didn't commingle, we coexisted. But if you ask my grandma Cathy, speaking their name is sacrilege. So I'd be lying to say that I didn't get a sick thrill knowing I was sleeping with the enemy. I know, I know, I'm a bastard.

I realize I haven't offered Rosalind any comfort, too lost in my own thoughts about our history and how this is going to affect my MC. Because it will. Mikey was the one who really enforced this treaty. With him gone, who knows what will happen.

"When is the funeral?" I ask, knowing my grandfather Johnny will want to show his respect to his old best friend. I don't think he ever recovered from the betrayal, and as much as he wanted to hate Mikey and Libby Rose, I know he really couldn't bring himself to do so.

"On Sunday," she replies with a sniffle. "What did you want to talk to me about?"

I pause. I may be a heartless bastard, but breaking up

with her while she already has tears in her eyes probably isn't the nicest thing to do.

"You're dumping me, aren't you?" she guesses, pursing her pink lips.

"You knew this wasn't going to last," I tell her, studying her profile.

Forbidden fruit always tastes better.

Fuck, I really am an asshole.

She gets out of the car without another word and slams the door behind her, the rose scent leaving with her. I know I shouldn't feel bad because she knew what this was, but there's a tiny slither of guilt that hits me anyway.

I head back to the clubhouse to tell my grandpa about his best friend's death.

You could hear a pin drop.

No one wants us at this funeral, yet just like I thought, Johnny had wanted to show his respect to a man he once loved like his brother. As we walk through the funeral home, all eyes are on us. I stand next to my father and grandfather; we're all dressed in black. This is the first time the Callistos and Montannas have been in the same room together in years, and will likely be the last. Rosalind is watching me with wide eyes from the front of the room, probably wondering with the rest of us how this is going to play out.

"We are here to simply show our respect to Mikey, and then we will leave," Johnny announces to Paulie, Rosalind's father and current president of the Angels MC. Paulie inherited the role when he married Mikey's daughter, since none of Mikey and Libby Rose's children were boys.

Paulie nods stiffly, telling his men to stand down,

and then turns back to the coffin where Mikey lies. One by one we go up and bow our heads, and then wait at the back of the room. Johnny goes last and lingers there for the longest.

As I'm walking away from the viewing, I can see an older woman. I'm assuming it is Mikey's widow, Libby Rose, since she's sitting front and center. She's dressed in all white. In fact all of the Angels MC is in white. I catch her eye, and she audibly gasps. I think I know why, because it's not the first time I've had that reaction. I know how much I resemble my grandpa. I can feel her eyes follow me as I walk to the back.

Just then a blonde woman walks in, the door clicking behind her. We lock eyes and hold. She's wearing a black suit, her small waist accented with a button in the middle, and her blue eyes are sad. As she keeps walking, she trips forward on her heels and I catch her, my arms automatically going around her.

We can't seem to look away from each other. She's beautiful, with plump, heart-shaped lips, almond eyes and a cute nose. She's the opposite of me with my dark hair, eyes and tan complexion. She smells like cherry blossoms.

"Thank you," she murmurs, removing her arm from my touch.

I stop and look around to see everyone staring at us. Everyone.

Grandpa Johnny eyes us both, shaking his head as if seeing a ghost, before approaching.

"What is it?" I ask him, but his eyes are on the woman next to me.

"You look so much like her," he says, staring in wonder.

The woman smiles, hiding her face. "I get told that all the time."

"What is your name?" he asks.

"I'm Julianna. I'm Libby and Mikey's granddaughter." She stares between Grandpa Johnny and myself. "You two are the spitting image of one another."

I've been told that my entire life. And then it all hits me.

This woman looks just like Libby Rose when she was younger, the woman Grandpa Johnny loved.

The woman who is sitting in the front row crying and looked at me with shock.

The same Libby Rose who left Grandpa Johnny for the man lying in the casket right now.

I can't let history repeat itself.

I walk by Julianna and to the door, Grandpa Johnny following behind me.

But unable to help myself, I take one last look at her before I walk out of the funeral home.

Julianna and Romeo.

How fucking tragic.

Chapter Two

Julianna

I had only just found out about my grandfather's passing. No one told me until I returned home from a business trip, because they hadn't wanted to upset me. Which actually pisses me off more. I'm extremely close to my grandparents, more than any of my siblings or cousins. I should've been notified.

And then on my way into the funeral, which no one told me that we were supposed to wear white to—I am in black—I tripped and landed in the arms of none other than Johnny "Romeo" Montanna, the man who is about to become president of the Devils MC.

Wonderful.

And he was good-looking too, what a waste.

I'll be the first to admit that I haven't been as involved in the club as I should have as the eldest daughter of the new president. Instead, I distracted myself with a business degree, which in turn will benefit the club, especially as I aim to take over the real estate side of things. But I haven't been as present as I should have been, with work trips like the one I was just on pulling me away.

At least I made it home for the funeral. And if I'm

being honest with myself, I like being away. It makes me forget about my life and responsibilities here.

Rosalind, one of my younger sisters, keeps glancing over at me.

"Are you okay?" I ask her.

She nods. "You and Romeo looked a little…close."

I purse my lips. "I've never even properly met him before. Why?"

She shrugs and looks out the car window while we wait for our other sister, Veronica. Being the eldest of three girls isn't for the faint of heart. Growing up, I was their second mother, manager and the one who got blamed for everything. Notice I didn't say best friend. We don't have that type of relationship.

"I don't know. He's about to take over as president for the Devils. He's basically your nemesis," she continues, sighing.

Whoever I marry will be the president of our MC, the Angels, since my parents have no sons. (Actually, none of the people in the Callisto bloodline have had boys. It's like the family was cursed with girls.) As a result, the women have to marry well to make sure that our MC runs accordingly. It's a lot of pressure on me, and a little outdated…okay, a lot outdated, but no one will listen to me. They don't think a woman can run an MC. And sure, back in the day MCs used to be all about putting on this macho front, but news flash, you want to know what MCs really do now? They make money, legally. I am in charge of managing over $50 million worth of properties and I'm looking to increase that by twenty-five percent. We are a business more than an MC, but if the men in my family want to convince themselves they are in a gang, they can.

But, as a result of the outdated patriarchal hierarchy, I've been promised to my father's second-in-command, his vice president, Victor, for as long as I can remember. Do I like it? No. Have I been trying to get out of it for years? Yes. He's a decade older than me, and I don't think I've ever seen the man smile. Ever. What I wouldn't give to have been born second or third. Rosalind and Veronica don't realize how good they have it.

"Who cares about Romeo?" I mutter, the intensity of his eyes flashing in my memory. I have bigger problems.

Veronica finally gets into the car, her floral dress flying everywhere from the wind before she closes the door. "Okay, let's get out of here. Grandma is still crying at the casket, but Mom said she will stay with her."

"Where's Dad?" Rosalind asks.

"He's rounding up everyone else to gather at the house. He asked that we get a head start and have the food set out."

I hesitate, feeling bad. I should be with Nanny. "Rosalind, maybe you go with Veronica and I'll wait with Nanny."

"She's fine," Veronica assures me before I'm able to leave the car. "Let her have her moment with Mom and the aunties."

I nod, knowing how close my mother and her sisters are, and reverse the car, taking us all back to our family home.

"So why didn't anyone tell me everyone was wearing white?" I ask, still annoyed that I stood out like a sore thumb and ended up matching with the Devils.

Rosalind looks up from her phone. "Didn't I?" she

says, but I can hear in her voice that she knows she didn't. Brat.

Victor is standing out front when I pull up to the clubhouse, and I take a moment to stare at him. He's strong and a protector, but I don't know. There's just something about him that I just can't put my finger on. Don't get me wrong, he's attractive enough, with his shaved head, dark brown eyes and heavily muscled physique. He just doesn't give me a spark.

The girls get out, while I linger, pretending to look for something in my handbag. The tension between us is slowly building because we both know what's going to happen soon.

And yeah, it's a little awkward.

Or maybe I'm just awkward, I don't know. We have barely ever kissed, so how am I supposed to sleep with him?

He comes over to the window, and I open the car door and slide out.

He's a loyal man who has worked hard and accomplished so much for the Angels, and although he's not who I would have chosen for myself, that doesn't mean something can't build here. We could have a good marriage, and be a strong unit and force for the MC. He has been groomed for his position in this, just like I have. I know I shouldn't believe in there being a soulmate or anyone like that. Nanny told me from a young age that the fairy tales I read about the girl finding her one true love are a myth. She said sometimes you need to make practical decisions and not let your heart rule. In fact, I think that is how she raised my mother and her sisters. I don't think I've ever seen true love in real life, only on TV. It's why I know I need to get over my hang-up about Victor and just accept the reality of the situation. I'll have a good life with Victor. We'll run the club together, he's promised me this.

"Anything I can do for you?" he asks, his voice low and deep. "Do you want to talk?"

His bald head shines in the sunlight, and for a second it's all I can focus on.

Victor is not one for emotions, or deep and meaningful conversations, so I appreciate the sentiment. Maybe because the time is fast approaching, and the two of us are going to have to find some common ground.

"I'm okay, but thank you, Victor. I think I'm just going to need some time to be alone for a little while." Although my parents don't like it, I got my own place away from the chaos. It's not far from here, but it's just for me, and although I do sometimes stay here in my childhood bedroom, I'm usually in my apartment.

He frowns, but nods. "You call me if you need anything," he adds, tapping on the hood of my car, and then turns back to walk into the house with my sisters, his broad shoulders blocking out the two of them.

We aren't just going to open up to each other like that overnight, and right now I don't have the energy. I sigh and gear up for a long day entertaining the masses.

When I get home, I lock the door behind me and head into my bathroom, staring into the mirror as I remove my diamond earrings, then tie my long blonde hair into a high bun. Taking off my shoes and suit, I glance back at my reflection and note how tired my blue eyes look. It's been a long day.

Turning on the shower, I let the steam fill the bathroom before I step under the scalding water. My granddad dying hurts a lot, and it's also a reminder that my time is nearing.

I try not to get my hair wet, but as usual it ends up damp anyway. I lean back against the glass as a thought hits me.

I'm going to be married soon.

Will Victor and I have wild, passionate sex? What if we don't ever have that chemistry? And if that's the case, shouldn't I be getting that out of my system now?

On the down-low, of course.

But I wouldn't be the only one. On the outside my world has so many rules, and everyone is so proper, but behind closed doors is a whole different story.

Everyone has a mask, and they are usually always wearing it.

Their skeletons are overflowing in their closets.

But me? I've always been a rule follower, for the most part. I had one secret boyfriend in high school, but my dad made me break up with him when he found out. I've always wanted to be a good older sister and lead by example. And after that I kind of buried myself in my studies. It's my fault, but it's not exactly fair though, is it?

With that thought in my mind, I get out of the shower, dry myself and climb onto the couch with a romance novel, wanting to escape reality for the rest of the day. This is the kind of love I want, the type I read about. High expectations, I know, because my family doesn't operate this way. I need to get over it.

But I mean, I could die tomorrow, and I don't want to leave this earth without experiencing different...things.

So why shouldn't I get to? I decide that I need to go to my special place.

Chapter Three

Romeo

"So Grandpa, what do you think my first order of business should be as president?" I ask, hoping to get some insight. Dad's fiftieth is coming up and I'll be taking over soon. As much as I knew this was coming, I can admit that I in no way feel ready for this.

"She looks exactly like Libby Rose back in the day," Grandpa Johnny says for the God knows how many times. "It took me back—I can't believe it. And Libby Rose herself has aged so beautifully. She hasn't changed much at all."

I roll my eyes. This again. It's been a day since the funeral, and he still can't stop talking about it.

"Grandpa Johnny, you know you can't keep repeating this over and over. Grandma is not going to like you talking about Libby Rose," I comment, picking up my whiskey from the bar and taking a sip.

Grandpa Johnny winces, knowing I'm right. And of course my grandma chooses that exact moment to step into the room, pausing as she hears my comment.

My grandmother is...rough around the edges. Not the picture of a loving grandmother, but rather a hard woman who leads by example. And she's very protective and possessive of my grandfather, so I know that I've just done him a disservice by saying what I said and having her hear it.

"Yes, our grandson is right," she says, pursing her lips. "I don't see why you need to mention her at all. You don't see me talking about all my ex-boyfriends."

"I know, I know, but I just never expected them to be so similar," he mutters.

"Why? Everyone says I look like you. Same deal," I say, then smile at Grandma. "And how are you?"

I try to change the subject, which she allows, but she is a little tense throughout the interaction. The truth is, Julianna is a beautiful woman, and I can tell why Grandpa Johnny was so devastated when Libby Rose left him, because she was obviously a blonde bombshell, too. She has that pinup girl, natural beauty good looks.

But there are plenty of pretty women out there. There's no point moping over just one. Women are replaceable. And trust me, I know, because I've worked through my fair share of them.

Grandma heads back into the kitchen after a quick conversation, leaving us alone in the lounge room once more.

"It just took me back, is all," Grandpa Johnny whispers, emotion flashing in his gaze.

Yeah, he can't seem to let this go.

Maybe he is the reason I won't allow myself to get too attached to any one woman. I've grown up seeing firsthand what it does to a man when it doesn't work out. I've seen how women can betray you, just like that.

And with your best friend?

Double whammy.

"Libby Rose didn't even look at me," he continues. "Mikey is dead now, and her eyes were still on him."

Oh, for fuck's sake.

"Come on, Grandpa, have a drink. There's no point looking to the past," I tell him, touching his shoulder.

Leaving him to his misery, I head outside to my Harley, grab my helmet and climb on. My bike is my happy place, and where I feel most at peace. A ride is just what I need right now.

After an hour riding around town, I make a stop to stretch my legs. I'm walking along when I see a woman. She's walking barefoot, shoes in hand, through the grass, and staring out at the sunshine, her long turquoise dress blowing all around her. I do what any mature man would do in this situation.

I ignore her. I have enough problems.

But on the way back to my motorcycle, I catch sight of her again, standing over the open hood of her car, staring down at the engine, clearly needing some assistance.

Jesus Christ.

I hesitate, then approach her. "Are you okay?"

She lifts those ocean-blue eyes to me; they widen when she realizes who I am. I know exactly who she is, too. "I'm fine, thank you."

Clearly.

"Do you want me to have a quick look?" I try again.

Her hands find her hips and she purses those heart-shaped lips of hers. "Romeo, right?"

"That's me," I reply.

I've barely seen this woman before and now I've seen her twice in two days. I know I should leave her alone, but fuck. Who am I to turn down a damsel in distress?

Especially one so pretty.

I'm unsure how she's related to Rosalind, but I know they have the same grandfather. Cousins, maybe? She looks different than Rosalind. Her features stand out more, her hair longer and a different shade. Rosalind is a platinum blonde, where Julianna is more of a sunshine blonde. More natural. And, of course, her blue eyes differ from Rosalind's brown.

I wonder if she knows about me and Rosalind. I'm guessing not.

"I appreciate you offering your help, but you're probably the last person I'd accept it from, so if you will be on your way, I'll handle this myself," she says as she pulls her phone out of the small handbag on her wrist.

She steps away with her phone to her ear and I can't seem to take my eyes off of her.

She's a walking red flag, yet all I can see right now is a carnival.

"You're stubborn, aren't you?" I mutter under my breath.

Her dad must not have answered her call, because her hand drops along with the phone and she scowls over at me. Not waiting for her to have her little tantrum, I check over the engine, and then open the driver's door and try to start the car.

"You have any jumper cables in the back?" I ask.

She shakes her head.

Her phone rings and I'm wondering if her family are going to help so I can leave, but when she starts talking her voice changes and becomes all professional, so it must be a business call.

"Yes, of course," she says, stepping away and turning her back to me for some privacy. "I'm glad they decided to accept my offer for five million."

This woman is closing a deal for five million?

Fuck.

She finishes up the call then turns back to me, while I'm still looking at her car and pretending I didn't overhear her conversation.

"Okay, so, your battery is dead. There's an auto parts store down the road—we can buy you what you need and get the car going again," I suggest, studying her. "Did you accidentally leave the lights on while you were on your walk?"

"I'm not sure. And why am I seeing you everywhere all of a sudden? Are you stalking me now?" she says, narrowing her gaze, putting her hands back on her hips.

"You wish," I reply, lips tightening. I am not my grandfather. I do not become putty over a woman. "Do you want me to help you, or not? Otherwise I'm heading home and you can wait here alone until you get in touch with your family."

I'm surprised they give her so much freedom. They must be getting soft. They didn't notice I had Rosalind in my back seat, and now they aren't even answering phone calls.

She sighs. "Okay, if you don't mind helping me." She pauses and then adds, "Please."

I hide my smile, because I know how much it must kill her to say that. "Come on."

When I nod to the back of my motorcycle, she winces. "Can you imagine what would happen if I'm seen on your back of your bike?"

"Tie your hair up; no one will know it's you."

She ties her long, beautiful blonde hair, grumbling

the entire time, puts my spare helmet on, then gets on behind me, her fingers gently touching my sides. She sits like a pro, someone who has grown up around motorcycles, and as I drive off and her body presses against mine, I know that I've made a critical mistake.

I like the way she feels against me a little too much, and I know that I can't have this one. One, I've already slept with her cousin, and two, it would cause way too much shit if it came out. We might not be at war now, but when our interests cross, we will have to face each other as enemies.

It's not a good idea to know how my enemy tastes.

We arrive at the auto parts store, and we walk in together and head to the front counter. I tell them what we need, they give it to us and, without thinking, I pay for it.

"Romeo, I can pay," she objects, waving her card around in front of me.

I ignore her, grab the jumper cables and head back out, pausing to admire some new riding gloves on the way, with her following behind me.

"You are infuriating, you know that? You don't even know me—why would you pay for that?" she asks, getting back on the bike. I can't wait to start riding back so I can't hear her.

"Don't worry about it" is all I say.

We head back to her car, and I get it up and running for her while she stands by, watching. I put the cables in her trunk in case she needs them again.

"All good to go," I say, leaving the engine on for her.

She opens her mouth, and then closes it. "Thank you," she finally says.

"No problem," I reply, smelling vanilla as she walks

past me to slide into the car. I spin around and head back to my bike.

"You know…" she starts. I turn back to her, seeing she's rolled her window halfway down, sunglasses on her face. "I think we're going to see a lot more of one another." She shines a smile. "Until next time."

Shit. Forbidden fruit needs to stop being so damn tempting.

Chapter Four

Julianna

Out of all the people that could have come to my aid, of course it had to be him. I don't like feeling like I owe anyone anything, and right now I feel like I owe him one.

And it makes me feel uneasy. And I don't like that I'm attracted to him either. He's hot. Like "make me wet by just smiling" kind of hot. Those smoldering chocolate-brown eyes do things to me, and paired with his flicked-back dark hair and his muscular build, I don't know many women who would turn that down. Jesus, who am I? I would never in a million years admit these thoughts out loud to anyone. I cannot have anything to do with him, and there I was flirting with him and promising I'll see him again. That is not me. I know I told myself that I needed to live a little before I married Victor, but it cannot be him.

I hate that he heard me discussing the new property I bought for the Angels MC, and how much we were spending, but at least he knows how successful our empire is, and that I'm the one calling the shots to keep it that way.

Maybe I could send him some thank-you chocolates

and call it a day. Or what else do playboys like? Alcohol? A packet of condoms?

I don't know.

But then it hits me.

I go back to the auto shop and buy those expensive riding gloves he was admiring, and wrap them up and mail them to his burlesque dancing club, Devil's Play.

There, now we're even, right?

The next day, Victor is standing out the front of my grandmother's house speaking to my dad when I pull up. I know I could call him and he would come running, but he's the last person I'd feel comfortable doing so.

"Julianna." My father smiles when I get out of the car. "I was just about to call you back from yesterday. Everything okay? I'm sorry I didn't—you know how busy it was with the funeral and all the people here. How did it go with the new property?"

"The deal is all sorted, the property is ours."

I give him a hug, my cheek against his expensive shirt. "And I called because I was having some car issues, but I got it sorted."

Kind of.

When I glance up at him, he's frowning. "Leave your car here and take one of mine. I'll get someone to look at it for you."

"It's okay, Dad. My mechanic already fixed it," I assure him, then look over at Victor, who is watching us. "Victor, how are you?"

"Good," he replies, nodding slightly. "You know you can always call me if you had any issues."

"I know. I didn't want to bother you," I lie.

He frowns. "That wouldn't be bothering me. That's my job."

His job.

Looks like he doesn't see this situation for anything other than it is, too. I suppose that's a good thing.

"My Julianna has a problem with asking for help," Dad gently chastises. "Your grandmother was asking for you."

"I know, that's why I'm here," I say, heading into the house. I can feel Victor's eyes on my back, and I wonder how easy my life would be if there was a spark between us.

But what's that saying?

Shit in one hand, want in the other. Let's see which one you get more of.

I find my grandmother in the kitchen, cooking dinner. She's one of those women who will always be beautiful, no matter her age, and when people tell me I look like her, I consider that a huge compliment. But Libby Rose is more than her looks. She's a warm, genuine, loving person. And people like that are hard to find. She's also one of the most intelligent people that I've ever known. She could have done anything she wanted in life, but raising her family was always most important to her.

"Hey, Nanny," I say, and she turns around and smiles. It doesn't reach her eyes, though, and I wonder if that spark will ever fully return with the love of her life now gone.

"There you are," she says, kissing me on both cheeks. "Come and help me make this pasta."

We work side by side in the kitchen, preparing the

meal with love. Like she has always said, that is the main ingredient.

"How are you doing?" I ask gently.

She turns to the pot, her back to me. "I'm fine, Julianna. All good things must come to an end, and we shared many, many happy years together. I can't complain. I need to be grateful for what time I had."

"Just because you're grieving doesn't mean you aren't grateful," I say softly. I want to ask her how it was seeing Johnny after all of these years, but I don't want to make her any more upset. The love triangle between them is a legendary story, one we all know about, but her true love was always Mikey. I think she loved Johnny but wasn't in love with him.

Like she can read my mind, she says, "I saw you talking to Johnny and Romeo at the funeral."

"Hardly," I reply in a dry tone. "I actually slipped and fell, and Romeo helped me up."

That's twice now he's come to my aid, the bastard.

With her giving me the opening, I ask the question I want to ask. "You didn't talk to him, did you?"

She shakes her head. "No. I knew he was there the second he stepped into the room, though."

"How?"

She smiles sadly. "I don't know. I could always sense Johnny's energy, and feel when he was near. But it was my husband's funeral—I wasn't going to make it about Johnny. I didn't want to face him and have to deal with all...that."

She stays quiet on the subject after that, and I'm more than happy for her to do so. We finish making dinner, and the whole family joins us to eat.

As I look around the table at my mother and father,

two sisters, grandmother and Victor, who somehow
gets invited to everything, I'm reminded of how much
I love each and every one of them. Well, minus Victor.
The members of the extended family were by earlier
in the day. Nanny has three other daughters and they
each have their own families.

I know I would disappoint them if I didn't fulfill my
duty, but I wonder if there's another way. Do I really
have to marry Victor? Surely there's a different scenario where everyone can win and get what they want.

Because as it stands, this isn't working for me.

"What are you thinking about so much?" Nanny asks
me, her blue eyes, the same ones only I inherited, gentle.

I glance around the table before replying. "Nothing."

"You can tell me," she replies quietly.

I shake my head and say nothing. She is the one I
would vent to, but now is not the time or place. I watch
Rosalind push the food around her plate and Veronica
make a joke with my mother. My father and Victor are
deep in talk, business as always.

"Maybe we should make a move on the Devils?" I
hear Victor say.

Frowning, I'm unable to stop myself from interject-
ing. "And why would we do that? We don't need to start
unnecessary drama." .

Both men look at me. "This doesn't involve you, Julianna," Victor grumbles.

I stare at him, tracing his profile with my gaze, and
wonder what he's going to look like naked. He takes
care of his body and is very muscular, and I know a lot
of women would love to be in my place. He has that
whole broad shoulders, bald-headed, alpha male thing
going on.

But he's wrong. Anything to do with our club involves me.

And he's going to have to accept me and my opinions.

Does he find me attractive? I never once thought about that, but I probably should if this is going to work between us. Or maybe our marriage will just be one of convenience.

I curse the last few generations of Callistos who haven't been able to produce a male heir. Maybe I'll be the first one to break the curse and have a boy, which would save any future daughters from going through an arranged marriage like myself. But my mother seems happy enough, I think.

Veronica taps Victor on the shoulder and says something that he laughs at. They have the easy friendship I've never had with him, maybe because they have no expectations there.

Sighing, I finish eating, and then help clean up before driving home.

All I know is that the decisions I make in the next few months are going to dictate the rest of my entire life.

No pressure, right?

Chapter Five

Romeo

"Hey, handsome," a woman purrs from behind me, pressing her breasts against my shoulder as she lowers herself onto the barstool.

I glance up from my drink long enough to let her know that I'm not interested. Devil's Play is one of the businesses we own, a bar and a burlesque club where we hang out regularly. I don't know if the woman works here, but she takes the hint and moves on. My grandfather never wanted to get into the strip club game. He says it's for amateurs. Instead, he opened other kinds of nighttime clubs and bars, none of which require women to be naked. He was smart like that, and as a result, we've never been investigated by the IRS or cops...at least for our businesses. Grandpa Johnny is all brains and class.

"I can't believe you're about to become the president of a fucking motorcycle club," River mutters, shaking his head before bringing his drink to his lips. River is one of the cousins I'm closest to, and I always knew he was going to be my right-hand man. I don't know if I fully trust anyone one hundred percent, but River is the closest it gets. If I was in trouble, he would be there and have my back no matter what. And I want him beside me throughout this new chapter in my life.

"I know," I admit, twirling the amber liquid around my glass. "I feel like we've been counting down to this for fucking years."

"Yeah, since we were twelve," he says with a lop-sided grin. "I remember when we went away to that cabin in the hills on holidays, we sat in the forest hiding because our parents were fighting about something, and we spoke about all the things that would change when you would become president."

I smile at the memory. "Yes, I believe no yelling at any of the children was the number one rule."

"That was Matthew's rule. He hated the yelling."

I remember that day—River, me and River's brother, Matthew, made sure we were scarce. Matthew and River's father, Robert, had drunk too much and was screaming at his wife, and my dad stepped in, trying to calm him down. Robert was known for his hot temper, and for not always treating his wife how he should.

And while River may also have a temper, I've never seen him mistreat a woman.

My eyes roam over his leather cut. He too will soon have a new patch to wear with pride: vice president. An MC is nothing without good men in the ranks. I know the older men are going to have some trepidation about me taking over, even though they knew it was coming. No one likes change, and when a new president steps up, there's a lot of it. I wouldn't want someone younger leading me either, but one day there will be.

My future son. And I want to leave behind a legacy for him.

Loyalty and money. That is all he is going to know.

And if I have a daughter, she's going to get the same treatment.

I've always known I was going to lead, and because of that I've thought long and hard about the Devils MC, and the type of president I was going to be long before I should have been worrying about those things.

"You still don't fuck the women here?" River asks, checking out one of the waitresses at the bar.

"Nope," I reply, my eyes following his. "I don't need that kind of trouble."

I know this would probably surprise people considering my reputation with women, but I prefer my dates a little more private. I don't fuck anyone who works for the MC. And I don't fuck women that have been with my MC brothers, and I know the performers and bar staff here love to fuck the men in the MC.

What can I say?

I'm an only child and I don't like to fucking share.

River smirks and tips the rest of his drink back, placing the glass back down on the bar louder than it needs to be. "You own this place now, Romeo. You can do anything you want."

My lip twitches. "With great power—"

"Comes great responsibility, I know. But you can still be responsible and have your fair share of pussy. Just wear a condom. Now *that* is responsible."

I laugh out loud. "Now tell me why the fuck I've chosen you to be my enforcer?"

"Because I have great fucking ideas," he replies, hailing down the waitress to order another drink. River might seem like a calm, easygoing kind of man, but I don't miss the way his eyes glance over the exits,

the people, and how he takes note of his surroundings.
There's another side to River that most don't see.

And they'd be thankful for that.

He's always on alert. He always knows where every
person in the room is. And he's someone you don't want
to get on their bad side. He's also the club's enforcer. So
when I'm with him, I'm able to relax, because I know
that nothing gets past him.

My phone beeps with another text from Rosalind.
I've been dodging her calls ever since we broke up, and
I have no intention of going back there. I'm a bit unsure
what she expects me to do. I was pretty clear we were
done and why. If I knew she was going to become that
clingy, I never would have slept with her in the first
place. Maybe I should just block her and be done with it.

My mind wanders to Julianna. It's been a week since
I helped her with her car, and I can't help but wonder
when I'm going to run into her next. I know, I know.
Forbidden fruit and all that shit. But she's so different
from Rosalind, and all the other women I've met before, in a pain-in-the-ass way. There's also something
about her that just makes me that little bit curious. Not
that I'd ever admit that out loud.

"You all good for a bit?" River asks, looking toward
the back rooms.

I nod. "Go ahead."

He grins, flashing his teeth, then jumps over the bar,
the waitress laughing and pulling him into the back with
her. Not unusual for River. The man is led by his dick,
but you know what, we all have our vices.

Echo, the manager here, approaches me. She's a beautiful woman, long red hair and green eyes. I've heard
some of the men here call her Jolene, like the Dolly Par-

ton song. The thing I like about Echo, though, is that she's strictly business. She's never once tried to hit on me. She does her job and looks after the staff, and we pay her well to do so.

She hands me a package. "This arrived here for you."

Frowning, I take it from her hands, inspecting the box. "I haven't ordered anything."

Turning it over, I see the sender's name and pause. What the hell is Julianna doing sending me something?

I decide to open it in private, and look back up at Echo.

She doesn't press, and instead looks over at the empty bar. "Where's Daisy?"

I simply raise my brows in response, and she frowns before moving behind the bar. We probably have an hour until the men start piling in, but she obviously doesn't want to risk it and leave the bar unattended, so she starts wiping glasses and keeping busy.

"How's everything been?" I ask.

She shrugs. "Good. We've had a few pretty insane nights. I'm glad you increased the security."

"Anything I should be worried about?"

"Well, after the last fight..."

When you mix men with big egos, alcohol and pretty women, there's always going to be some trouble. But it's been getting progressively worse. Last week, let's just say that shit got violent real quick. We don't typically get many Callistos in to see any of the shows, but when we do, there's always some bullshit, and someone usually gets hurt. Normally they just get rowdy, since this is not a strip club, but a couple of the guys got handsy with the waitresses and my men do not tolerate that kind of disrespect. We may be part of an MC, but we have a code—don't be an asshole when it's not necessary and don't stand by while other men are assholes. Seems common sense to me, but society goes backward sometimes and the most basic act of decency is ignored.

"Anything you need, you let us know," I say, studying her.

She smiles. "I know. How does it feel, by the way?"

"How does what feel?"

"About to be running shit. Being in charge. All the responsibility. You can't just run around as the heir having your fun." She starts rearranging the bottles of alcohol.

I think about the question. "It feels...the same. But then I have these moments where I feel the weight of everything on my shoulders. If I'm being honest..." I haven't voiced this out loud yet. "I have been preparing for this my whole life, but I have no idea what I'm supposed to do."

It feels good to finally say that. This role has been something I've always known I was to inherit, but it's so unlike other MCs. With us the presidency is inherited. The club members are all family or longtime friends, and we all have such loyalty for each other. And the money isn't bad either.

Moans start from the back room and continue to get louder, and the two of us share a laugh. "At least someone is having some fun around here," she mutters.

"What? No one you have your eye on?"

She huffs. "I want a man who doesn't spend all his time at a burlesque club, except I spend all my damn time at a burlesque club, so..."

My lip twitches. "Quite the conundrum."

"You have no idea," she replies in a dry tone. "But

hey..." She reaches over to touch my forearm. "I'm sure it's like everything. You fake it until you make it."

I laugh. Echo is good people. She has a business degree and is probably overqualified to work here, yet she chooses to stay, and I pay her well for it.

River makes an appearance, dark hair all mussed, expression satisfied. "What did I miss?" he asks, glancing between the two of us.

"Not much can happen in a minute," Echo fires back, keeping a straight face.

River simply grins, while I laugh at her quick wit. While he can be quick to temper, I've never seen him lose it at a woman. If a man had made that joke, I don't know if it would have had the same outcome.

The club starts to fill out, and more staff arrive to accommodate. River and I have another drink and make sure that everything is running smoothly with security before we head out. Our number one priority is making sure the women are safe, and we hire the best men in the business to do so, the men from the MC stepping in when need be.

We get on our Harleys and ride back to the clubhouse. While I haven't officially been sworn in as president yet, the men all know it's coming and the vibe in the clubhouse has changed. I can feel it the second I walk inside. My dad is having a drink at the bar, a few men standing around him. He smiles when he sees me.

"There he is," he says, drink in hand. "How's everything at Devil's Play?"

"Good," I say, sitting next to him. He's been sending me to all of our businesses without him so I can make my own connections with the people involved. Especially in our construction business, which brings in the most income. The bars and clubs are a close second. But I've been with him and watching him run everything since I can remember. I know what I'm doing with the businesses. I'm not nervous about that. I'm good with money, and I know how to make money. It's the people that are another story. And another issue for us will be that the debt tax from the Angels MC will soon cease, so we'll need to cover that with more income. But one problem at a time.

He pours a drink and hands it to me, while River heads outside where the rest of the men are partying.

"You're ready for this," Dad states, nodding as he lifts his glass to mine. "It's almost time to make it official."

Fuck.

It's actually happening.

Later, when I'm alone in my room, I open the package from Julianna. It's the riding gloves that I was looking at at the auto shop. Damn, that woman doesn't miss a beat.

The attached note says: *Thank you for your help. Let's call it even.*

I can't help it, I laugh to myself. She's got too much pride for her own good.

But I don't have time to think about Julianna.

My father is stepping down as the president of the Devils MC.

And his legacy?

Will now all fall on me.

Chapter Six

Julianna

"Where are you off to?" Victor asks as I step outside after dinner, startling me. He's standing in the dark to the right of me, smoking a cigarette. I feel on edge when he's around, and I don't know why.

"Shit, you scared me," I mutter, hand going to my heart. When he says nothing else, I continue. "I'm heading home. This will go on all night, and I have a lot to do tomorrow."

I unlock my car door and move to open it, but he puts his hand on the window, resting his large body against it. "Before you go, I think we need to have a talk."

"About what?" I ask, lifting my face to him.

But I know what.

"What" has been a big elephant in the room between us ever since I found out that one day he's going to be my husband.

"Your father wants to speak to us tomorrow," he says, and dread fills my stomach.

"Has he set a date that he's going to step down?" I ask, even though I already know the answer. He has. And the time for him to marry me off is now.

He nods. "He wants to tell us together. Listen, Julianna, I know we won't have a loving marriage, but we could still have a good one where we respect each other. That's more than what some people have. I really want this, and I'm not going to let anything stand in the way of me becoming the next president."

He started off rather sweet, but I see his last line for what it is.

A threat.

Any hope of us having a proper marriage just flew out the window.

He's not going to let me stop him getting what he wants. However, in this moment I realize that I'm not going to let him do the same. If I'm going to be part of this, I need to ensure I get what I want.

"I hear you, Victor. Loud and clear," I reply, putting my hand on the door handle once more. "And I'll see you and my father tomorrow."

He takes the hint and backs away, watching me get into my car and speed off as quickly as I can. As much as I don't want a marriage without love, I think respect is more important. Especially in our world.

But I also want more.

I want passion, connection and adventure.

And he sure as hell isn't going to give me that.

When I get home, I call my father and ask him if he can come and see me tomorrow morning. He agrees. My only chance to sway him is going to be if I get him alone, away from Victor. I'm about to call it a night when my cousin Bella sends me a text, asking if I want to meet her out for a drink.

She names one of our usual spots, a bar called Damage, and I throw on some red lipstick and Valentino perfume and get back into my car. A drink with someone I trust sounds like the therapy that I need right now.

She's sitting at the bar, her long dark hair instantly recognizable. She turns, her beautiful profile on display, smiling when she sees me. She stands up and we hug before settling back down on the barstools. Bella is my cousin on my mother's side, although she has taken after her father's side with her looks.

"How are you?" I ask, placing my bag down on the counter.

"Not too bad. I have to admit I was surprised but happy that you said you'd come out," she says, sighing. "I was stood up on a date, but I didn't want to go home, so I thought I'd try my luck."

My brow furrows, instantly feeling protective of her. "Who in their right mind would stand you up? Look at you."

"Online dating," she murmurs, shrugging. "You are going to be better company anyway. What do you want to drink? Margarita?"

"Sounds perfect." She orders the first round, and I basically inhale it. "Okay, I know why I'm feeling shitty tonight, but what's with you? You look like you needed that drink more than me."

"It's time," I say, licking the salt from my lips. "Time for me to marry Victor."

Her gray eyes widen. "Fuck."

"Fuck is right."

"I'm sorry, Julianna. Is there anything you can do?" she asks, but the sadness in her eyes tells me that she knows the answer to that. Our family is so big, and so full of women, that I don't really have any friends outside of my family. And Bella is my favorite cousin. My favorite cousin who knows everything that is coming my way. The plank I'm supposed to walk. "Besides drink yourself into a stupor."

"I'm going to speak to my dad tomorrow, but I can imagine how that will go down," I say softly, looking toward the bar for more alcohol.

"Things can change. Someone just needs to instigate that change," she says, reaching out and touching my arm. "If you want to run away, I hear that Sri Lanka is really beautiful."

I laugh. "I'm not leaving my birthright. This doesn't belong to Victor—it belongs to me. But it might come to that. Who knows? I've always known about Victor, but tonight, hearing him say that the time is fast approaching, it just made me panic. Like I felt sick in my stomach. I thought I had prepared myself, but apparently that's not true."

"You following me or something?" suddenly comes a deep voice from next to me. I turn and look into brown eyes and a cocky smile.

Shit.

"This is my bar," I announce. "Shouldn't you be on your side of town, or at one of your clubs?"

He laughs, and it's a nice sound. "There's no visible line of what's mine and yours. I'm just here for a drink. I'm sure we can get along long enough for me to make that happen."

A man comes up behind him, his blue eyes widening as they land on me. "I'm...fuck."

"Nice to meet you, Fuck," I say in a dry tone, and Romeo laughs some more.

"This is River," he says, nodding at his friend. River is a good-looking man, about Romeo's height but leaner.

There's a glint in his eyes that I've seen before and recognize. This man is a killer. But he covers it well with his easy smile and demeanor.

He turns to Bella and smiles. "And who are you?"

"I'm Bella," she says, looking between River and me.

"You're not a Callisto, are you?" he asks, tone hopeful.

"Sorry to disappoint," she replies, with a sexy smirk.

"Ah, fuck," he mutters, but still sits down next to her. "Guess we are all making bad decisions tonight. Can I buy you a drink?"

I turn back to Romeo to find his eyes already on me. "Drink?"

"I need one, but I'm buying," I reply. "What do you want?"

He arches his brow. "Do the Angels not pay for their women? You should be used to it."

I purse my lips. "But you aren't an Angel, are you? The rules are a little different here. And I don't feel like owing you anything."

"You don't owe me anything, Julianna. It's a drink, for Christ's sake," he says, ordering himself a whiskey and me another margarita. With Bella and River chatting between themselves, Romeo and I are left to do the same. He smells so damn good; I don't know what cologne he wears, but it should be illegal. The spicy, almost woody scent taking over my common sense.

"What cologne do you wear?" I ask.

"Issey Miyake. Why?"

"No reason," I reply, thanking the waitress when she places my drink in front of me. "Is my cousin okay with him?"

"Are you okay with me?" he asks, lip twitching.

I just give him a "don't fuck with me" look, and he laughs.

"Probably not, but they are grown adults," he replies, amusement in his tone.

Sighing, I silently agree and lift the cocktail up to meet his glass. "Thank you."

"You're welcome," he says, moving closer to me. "It's funny you ask about my cologne, because I can smell your vanilla scent every time I'm around you. And I think I like it a little too much."

Our eyes lock and hold. I do wear vanilla as my signature scent, and I like that he's noticed that. As I take a sip from my drink, he watches with an intensity that thrills me when I lick the salt from my bottom lip. His eyes flare ever so slightly.

Fucking hell.

"So, Julianna. You're the heir to the Angel throne. How does it feel?"

I realize in that moment that Romeo is probably one of the only people to know how I feel. So I decide to be honest.

"It's surreal, anticlimactic and daunting." I take a big gulp of my drink.

He stares at me for a few seconds without blinking. "I like the honesty. Are you always this blunt?" he finally asks.

I shrug. I think the alcohol is hitting me. "Nope." I pop the "p."

He smiles and it's uninhibited, reaching all the way to his eyes. When he smiles like that it's like I see him in a different light. He's not the president of the Devils MC. He's Johnny Montanna. I'm rendered speechless.

"Well, I'll tell you a secret," he says as he leans in,

his lips right by my ear. When he speaks, I visibly shudder throughout my body. "I feel the exact same, but I'll deny it if you ever repeat that."

He pulls away, and it takes everything in my body not to force him back toward me and wrap my arms around him, breathing in his scent.

In my current headspace, being around Romeo is the worst idea ever. Yet my feet won't seem to move to take me away from him.

"I won't repeat anything—your secret is safe with me. In fact, I'll deny ever even speaking to you," I say with a cheeky grin.

He laughs, eyes hooded. "That's probably smart."

"What can I say, I'm an intellectual woman—"

"And very modest, clearly," he interjects.

I tuck my hair back behind my ear. "Modesty gets a woman nowhere in my world, Romeo."

"Our world," he corrects, our eyes connecting and holding.

"Julianna, are you okay?" Bella asks, looking at me from around River's big head.

I nod. "Are you?"

She nods too, but her eyes are a little wide, like she knows we should not be here right now, yet none of us is making the move to get the hell out of here. It's like we are waiting for one of us to muster up some common sense but we're both coming up short.

"We are both right here, you know," River states, and when Bella turns her head to look away, he quickly lifts her hair to his nose and smells it.

"There's something wrong with your friend," I tell Romeo, blinking slowly.

His lip twitches. "I know. And he's my cousin."

"Bella—"

He turns my face to his with his fingers on my chin. "Nothing will happen to her, I promise."

"And what about me?" I ask, swallowing hard.

He licks his lips. "I definitely won't let anything happen to you, Julianna."

His thumb strokes my cheek before he lets me go, and my skin tingles where he touched me. My heart is racing, and I feel so fucking alive right now. Why can't Victor make me feel this way? Why does Johnny "Romeo" Montanna?

"Do you want to get out of here?" I ask, the thought of my future husband making me feel bold.

"Where do you want to go?" he asks, standing up and throwing some money down on the bar.

I step around River to get to Bella. "I'm getting out of here—you coming?"

Her brow furrows, and she grabs my arm and pulls me away from them. "What are you doing?"

"I'm going to have a little fun before I might have to sell my soul," I reply, glancing back and seeing both the men watching us like hawks. "And that guy is dangerous. I caught him smelling your hair."

"And you think Romeo fucking Montanna isn't dangerous?" she whisper-yells.

"I've had a few interactions with him," I say with a shrug. "I don't know. I don't need your judgment right now."

"No judgment, I just don't want you to do anything that you'll regret."

"I'll regret it if I don't," I say, and she nods.

"I'm going to stay here with River. Text me when you get home safe."

I look into her eyes. "Oh my God, we are both idiots."

She laughs. "You only live once, right?"

"Are you sure you want to be alone with him? We can drop you off on the way."

She glances back at River. "He won't hurt me."

"Bella—"

"I'll be fine."

Sighing, I nod. "Okay." I kiss her on her cheek and head back over to Romeo, stopping by River on the way. "You better look after her and get her home safe."

"He will," Romeo says from behind, the threat in his voice clear. "Won't you, River?"

River nods and smiles at Bella. "Of course."

I leave with Romeo, hoping like hell no one sees us together, and get onto the back of his bike. He only had one drink, and I had two; I can't imagine that he's over the limit.

I enjoy the ride, the wind on my face, and being pressed up against his leather jacket. I forget all of my problems and just live in the now, and it feels so fucking good.

He parks his bike in front of a big house. "Where are we?" I ask, as he helps me off the bike.

"My house," he replies, undoing the clasp on my helmet and placing it on the back of his bike. "I barely come here, but it's a safe space when I need a break from the clubhouse."

"It's beautiful," I say, admiring the two-story, newly built home.

"Yes, it is," he replies, and leads me to his front porch.

The minute we get through the door, I turn to see he's looking at me. Without thinking, I lean forward to kiss him, and he must have been waiting for me to give him the signal, because as soon as my lips touch his, he takes control, pushing me back against the wall and kissing me deeply.

The keys in his hand drop to the floor as he lifts me up and I wrap my legs around him. His mouth moves down my jawline and to my neck, and a loud moan escapes my lips.

This seems to wake us up from our stupor, and he locks the front door with me still in his arms. He carries me to his bedroom and all but throws me down on the king-size mattress. As he starts to pull off his shirt, revealing thick arms, ripped abs and those sexy Vs on his hips, I have a moment of clarity.

Am I really doing this?

And then his pants come off, exposing a big, beautiful erection, and I forget about anything else.

"Okay, wow," I whisper to myself, and as he laughs, it jiggles, and I can't seem to take my eyes off it.

No wonder he is such a cocky bastard.

I might not have as much experience as him, but I wrap my fingers around him and start to stroke gently, staring up at him to gauge his reaction. By the tenseness in his jaw and the lust in his eyes, I'd say he likes what I'm doing.

I take the head into my mouth and suck, watching as his eyes close in pleasure.

I feel powerful in this moment.

"Fuck," he grits out between clenched teeth.

I smile around his cock.

Chapter Seven

Romeo

Her shy little touches and licks are going to be my un-doing. She keeps sucking the head of my cock into her sweet mouth, with just enough pressure to drive me crazy. I know we shouldn't be here right now. She shouldn't even know where my personal home is, never mind being inside it with her mouth on me, but knowing that makes it even hotter. There's just something about her, I can't explain it, but I've never been so hard in my entire fucking life and I'm about to come in her mouth before I can even get inside of her pussy.

She takes as much of me into her as she can, then bobs up and down. My fingers tangle in her hair, but I let her take the lead until I physically can't take any more.

"Lie back," I demand, and she listens like a good girl, while I lift up her dress and pull down her panties. I kiss up her thighs, and she moans while I take my time, teasing her until I finally spread them apart and lower my mouth to her pussy.

"Oh my God," she breathes as I slowly lick her, tasting her and loving every second of it. She's so sweet and wet and...perfect. I've always been a man who loved going down on a woman, but never this much.

"Romeo," she moans, lifting up her hips and encouraging me, wanting more.

Knees on the floor, I lean forward so I can get even more of her, licking her clit until she comes, getting louder and louder as each wave of pleasure hits her. Only when she sags back against the mattress, completely satisfied, do I strip her down naked and take a quick moment to admire her body. Her breasts are fucking amazing, round and heavy, her nipples pink and pointed right at me. Unable to help myself, I lower my head for a taste. She moans and strokes my hair. I hear my phone vibrating in the background, but I ignore it. Whatever it is can fucking wait.

"You are beautiful," I manage to get out, grabbing a condom from my bedside table and sliding it on. She spreads her thighs and beckons me with her finger. With a grin, I mount her, and kiss her deeply as I slide inside of her, slowly. She's drenched, and feels so fucking good. This might be the only time we have together, so I want to make the most of it. I want to fuck her in every position I can think of.

After a few minutes I pull out and roll her onto her stomach, fucking her from behind. My fingers grip her ass cheeks, before I reach down between her thighs to play with her clit. She's so wet and sweet, and as she lifts her head back I bend down to kiss her, still moving deep inside of her.

I then lean back and pull her up so she's sitting up on me, my chest against her back, and kiss the side of her neck, running my teeth along her soft skin. I'm not gentle, but I can tell that she likes that by her moans and the way she pushes toward me, begging for more. You can always sense what a woman wants and needs if you pay attention. And I do. To every gasp, every moan.

She stiffens slightly when my finger slides a little farther upward, so I take the hint and focus on other things, my hands moving to grip onto her hips as I thrust.

"Romeo," she whispers, turning her sweet mouth for another kiss.

I move harder, deeper, and she moans out in pleasure, urging me on.

I make her come again before I finish, and when I do it's with her on top of me, her blue eyes looking into mine. She's a little shy and glances down, but brings her gaze back to mine as I finish, as if she's unable to look away.

We lie side by side panting afterward, both of us staring at the ceiling. I wonder if, like me, she's contemplating her life choices.

I just fucked the woman who is my enemy. The woman whose family broke my grandfather's heart.

And it was the best sex I've ever fucking had.

I turn to her and take her hand in mine. "You okay?"

She nods and flashes me a smile.

I bring her knuckles to my lips and kiss them, and then go and get us both some water. Julianna is leaving my bathroom when I get back, and bends down to pick up her clothing off the floor. I stop in my tracks and just admire the view.

She turns and catches me staring. "You all right there?"

"Uh-huh," I mutter, and hand her the bottle of water. "Can I get you anything? Food? Do you want to have a shower?"

She sits down on the bed and opens the bottle, taking a sip. "A shower would be good. Will you be joining me?"

My eyebrows rise. I would have thought she'd had enough of me by now, but apparently not. "Do you want me to?"

She stands and offers me her hand, and I take the invitation.

In the shower we wash each other, and then our hands start to roam.

She's insatiable.

And so am I.

I lift her up against the tiles and slide into her. "Fucking hell, Julianna," I say into her ear, biting down on the lobe. "You're going to be the death of me, you know that?"

And not in the way I would have thought.

"The feeling is mutual." Everyone wants our motorcycle clubs to get along, right?

This is us getting along. Really fucking well, as a matter of fact.

I mean, no one else needs to know about this. It can be just our secret.

It makes it even more exciting.

I've had many one-night stands in my time, but this feels different. Julianna is...something else.

We finish up in the shower, dry ourselves and jump back in bed, both of us falling asleep in exhaustion.

It's the best sleep I've ever had.

Chapter Eight

Julianna

I wake up naked and wrapped in Romeo, with him spooning me, his arms and legs draped over mine. The sun streaming in lets me know it's morning and that I should probably get my ass up and home. After gently pushing him off me, I grab my clothes and start sliding them on.

Last night was…yeah, not my best idea, yet the best night ever. Romeo was so good in bed; he obviously has a lot of experience, because the man knew what he was doing. I don't think I've ever felt so good. He's going to be a hard act to follow, that's for sure.

I might not have slept with many men, but I don't think many of them are so generous. He read my body and gave me what I liked, and he took his time with it. If most men were like that, women wouldn't stop talking about it, and I doubt they'd be complaining about having to be intimate with their husbands.

Bella texts me, asking how the night went. She assures me River was nothing but a gentleman. I reply and let her know I had a good night, and that I'll catch up with her soon.

Once I'm fully dressed, I glance down at Romeo, who is still fast asleep. I'm not sure about the protocol here— do I just slip away without saying anything? I decide to leave a little note next to his bed, writing it on one of the Post-it notes I always carry in my handbag. My fingers linger above the paper, not sure what to write, but I decide on something a little funny instead of cute. I jot down my phone number and add a little 10/10 rating.

I stick the note on his bedside table, and then get the hell out of there. I order an Uber from the shops just near his house. When I arrive home and see my dad's car out the front, only then do I remember that I told him to meet me here so I can talk about Victor.

Fucking hell.

I'm doing the walk of shame right into him.

He gets out of his car as I get out of the Uber, and I know that I'm in deep shit right now.

"Where have you been?" he asks, while I look for my key in my handbag.

"I went out with Bella and crashed with her." I mean, half of that is true.

He stays quiet until we get inside and sit on my couch.

"You're out partying, Julianna? What is going on with you?" he asks, brow furrowing. He looks concerned, and disappointed. I've always been the golden child and have never stepped out of line, except for that one boyfriend in high school, but my sisters were caught doing that, too. Aside from that, I always listen to my family. I'm respectful. But what I'm about to tell him I know that he isn't going to like. I decide to go with some honesty.

"I had a few too many drinks with Bella, and yes, I think that might be because I'm struggling a little bit right now, Dad. That's why I wanted to talk to you," I say, shifting on the leather.

I do feel like crap, sitting here with Romeo's scent still on me, but that can't stop me from what I'm about to say. In fact, it only proves even further that marrying Victor is not right for me.

"What is it?" he asks gently. I can tell that he's worried, and I hope that means he will actually listen to what I'm about to say. "Are you okay? Is business okay?"

Business. Of course.

That is a safe conversation between us.

I wouldn't say that I'm emotionally close to my dad. On the outside, it might look like we have a good relationship, but deep down I'm well aware that I'm not his first priority. I know he loves me, of course, but he loves what I can do for the MC even more. I'm just a cog in his machine. So although he does love me, that love comes with conditions.

It's how he feels about my mother, too. They are the perfect example of why an arranged marriage does not make for a happy life. I've heard stories about my mother, Jenny Belle, when she was young. The firstborn daughter of Libby Rose and Mikey Callisto. She was vibrant and adventurous and wild and free. But ever since I can remember, she's not been the woman I heard about or saw in the pictures. We were close enough when I was growing up, but all my life she's been quiet and kept to herself. I think marrying my father dulled her flame and I will not let the same thing happen to me.

"Business is going well. The tax debt will be ending soon, so I think we should invest that extra money into a new business venture. I have some other ideas..."

"You just keep your mind on the real estate. That's what you're good at."

I sigh. Okay, then.

"Victor said you wanted to talk to us, so I'm assuming you're expecting us to get married soon," I blurt out, licking my suddenly dry lips.

Lips that were just all over Romeo's cock.

Fuck.

At hearing Victor's name, my dad's eyes harden and his expression is devoid of emotion. Not a good sign for me wanting him to try to see things from my side of the story. I should have known I wouldn't get the reaction that I'd like from him, but I at least thought he'd listen to how I feel.

"Yes, and you knew this was happening. As per tradition, it's time for me to step down, and the Angels MC needs Victor to lead them, with you at his side. He's going to be a good president, and together you will make a great team. I chose him for you because of how capable he is. He will look after you and never let anything happen to you. He would protect you with his life."

"I don't want to marry Victor," I declare, wrapping my arms around myself. "Victor might be perfect for the Angels, but that doesn't mean he will be the perfect husband for me."

"It has long been decided, Julianna," Dad growls, losing his patience with this conversation. "And I thought that you understood how important your role is for our future. It's our family's tradition. It always has been and always will."

Our family's tradition. My family. Not Victor's. Not even my father's. The women of the Callisto family are the true Callistos.

"I can lead the MC without Victor," I say unexpectedly. "I don't need him. It is my birthright, not his, and I don't need someone to look after me. I don't need someone to protect me. I run the entire real estate business for the MC. Our portfolio of property is over $70 million because of me, and I can grow it further. I can make more money for the MC and build a real estate empire. Just because I don't have a penis, I can't lead? We are close to a $100 million company! He's just the muscle, and I can find muscle anywhere. Let me do it."

I'm giving voice to something I've thought about for a while. This is mine and I will not let some man come in and take over. But the look on my father's face tells me he's not impressed.

"Julianna, Victor is much more than muscle. He's been preparing for this role for years, and you know a woman cannot be president. What MC has a female president? It's just the way things are done. Your role is still just as important, but the men won't respect a woman leading them. I don't understand why you are questioning all of this now, right when it's time for me to step down. I don't need this stress, Julianna."

He doesn't need this stress?

How about I sell him off like a piece of meat?

Oh, that's right, he's a man. Such patriarchal bullshit.

He doesn't have to worry about things like this.

"Let me ask you this, Dad. Other than the fact that you all ride motorcycles, what is it about the Angels that make you an MC? The Angels are a business organization. We have real estate, which I manage, and all the females in this family have their own role, yet the men do what? What do the men do to contribute?"

I can see my father's face get red, and I think I crossed

a line. Hit a nerve. Maybe even told the truth that every-one refuses to see.

"Julianna, that is enough. You will not lead the An-gels. Victor will," he spits out.

Realizing he's not going to change his mind, I de-cide to try a different tactic. "Okay. What if I ask for more time to get to know Victor better, on more than a friendship level?" I lie. "I just need a little more time. Don't you want me to find love, Dad?"

He tilts his head and studies me for a moment, then nods. "Yes. Okay. I only want my girls to be secure. Look at your mother and me. It took a while, but we have love for one another. If this is what you need, I can give you two more time so you can date and get to know each other."

I let out a breath I've been holding. Maybe he does understand me. Maybe he really does want me to find love. Maybe he—

"But this is happening, Julianna. I will not change my mind." He stands up to leave. "I'll let Victor know. He won't be happy because it postpones him getting sworn in as president, but he will understand. I don't want you avoiding him, though, Julianna. This isn't going away, so I think you should embrace it. I'm set-ting you up to have a good life. You will never have to want for anything."

Except a man I might actually love.

Oh, and freedom and free will.

You know, things other people take for granted.

Also, I honestly don't think my father knows how capable I am. Whenever I go over projects with him, he placates me and just yeses me to death. How is it the twenty-first century and yet I feel like it's still the 1700s when it comes to a woman's place in the family?

My father gets in his car and drives off. I forgot to mention that he hasn't been on his motorcycle in five years since he was in a bike accident. Yes, the president of the Angels MC doesn't ride a bike. The irony is not lost on me.

I don't know how much time I've bought myself, but it's going to have to be enough.

Because I'm not going to marry a man I don't love. So help me God.

Chapter Nine

Romeo

When I wake up I know instantly I'm alone in my bed. I should be thankful she decided to leave so we don't have to deal with the awkward morning after a one-night stand, but I kind of wish she'd stayed for another round.

Sliding out of bed, I laugh to myself when I see her note. A ten out of ten. I would give her the same. I save her number in my phone and then hop in the shower, thinking about the night before. I never expected it to take the turn that it did, but I have no regrets, and I hope she feels the same.

Once I'm dressed and ready to face the day, I send her a quick text.

Romeo: You get home safe? You know I would have dropped you home, right?

Julianna: That wouldn't have been the best idea. Especially considering my dad was at my house when I got there.

Shit.

Yeah, not the best idea.

That likely would have started an all-out war between our two motorcycle clubs, and we don't really want that.

Still, I don't feel like much of a gentleman with her leaving on her own the way she did.

Romeo: Okay, good point. Next time wake me up, though, and I can make sure you get there safely. I'll wear a costume and drive a stolen car if I have to.

Julianna: Next time?

I grin as I type out the reply.

Romeo: Yeah, next time. I'd like that, wouldn't you?

I see the three dots indicating that she's responding, but nothing comes. Fuck. I feel like a teenage girl who just told her crush she liked them and now I'm waiting for a response that never comes. She finally replies.

Julianna: Tonight?

Romeo: Fuck yes.

My cousin Matthew is out the front working on his bike when I get to the clubhouse. Matthew is River's younger brother. And when I say younger, I mean like Irish twins—they are about eleven months apart. They couldn't be more different, in looks and personality. River and I look a bit alike, with dark features, but he doesn't resemble our grandpa as much as I do. He hides a darkness and brutal streak, while Matthew has a heart of gold and is full of humor and laughter. He takes after his mother, with brown curls and hazel eyes. They're complete opposites, but I love them both equally. We grew up as brothers.

"Hey," I say as I take off my helmet. "You need a hand?"

He glances up, hazel eyes warm. "Hey, Romeo. Or should I say Prez?"

"Not yet, but very soon." I grin.

Matthew nods to his bike. "She's giving me some trouble."

"Let me have a look." I'm a mechanic by trade, and I love fixing bikes and cars. I also love just talking shit with my family now and again, without taking everything too seriously. I probably don't have any best friends because I'm always with my family. And to me, family always comes first.

"Where were you last night?" he asks casually, while I start looking over the bike.

I still. "What do you mean?"

"River came in about midnight, and you were missing in action. He tried to call you—some shit went down at Devil's Play, but he handled it."

I guess River did not get laid last night, then, and that was likely him calling me on the phone while I was.

"Fight broke out, usual bullshit. Callistos decided to see a show," he explains, and I frown. They usually leave Devil's Play alone, but they've been showing up more and more recently. Maybe they are starting to feel a little bold with a new president about to step in from both MCs. No one likes change. While I can respect their position, I am pissed about the execution.

Meanwhile I had my cock in the Callisto princess last night.

What a fucking disaster.

"A few of the men didn't like that you were unreachable," he adds, voice low. "They're looking for anything they can use right now, so be careful."

Fuck me. "I'll bet," I say, jaw clenching. My own men are testing me.

"Good night, though?" he asks, smirking.

"It was." Too fucking good.

"You ever going to bring one of those women here for us to meet?"

"Only if I plan on marrying her," I admit, inspecting the engine. "And for that to happen, she is going to have to be one hell of a woman."

And preferably someone my family would approve of.

"I think you should be more worried about what woman would want to marry you," Matthew replies, chuckling at his own joke.

I arch my brow. "I'm about to be president."

He tilts his head and runs his hand over his curls. "Yeah, you're right. Women love that shit. But do you want the woman you marry to love that shit?"

Matthew is always saying shit like this. Philosophical, smart shit. He sees things many do not.

"As if you aren't using that cut to get laid."

He smiles widely. "I was, and I did. But getting laid gets old. I'm talking soulmate shit."

"Did you hit your head? You feeling all right?"

He shrugs, a sheepish smile on his face. "I'm dating someone now. She's really cool; I think you'll like her. These women who love the cut, they aren't wife material.

I think you know that. It's why you keep your personal life completely separate from the club."

My cousin, unlike most of the men I'm used to, is a genuinely good person. He's the boy-next-door type. I don't know if he was meant to be in an MC; he seems more like a doctor or psychologist. He's very much like his mother, my aunt Lisa. She's my favorite aunt and more of a mother to me than my own. But sometimes life chooses your ending for you, and in our case, it was chosen before we even entered this world. We are Devils, whether we like it or not.

"I can't wait to meet her" is all I say, knowing how right he is.

We fix up his bike and then I head inside and ask the men if they want to go on a ride.

But in the back of my mind, all I'm thinking about is tonight when I can have Julianna back under me.

An Uber drops Julianna off—I'm guessing it's safer that way so no one can see her car parked out front. I open the door before she can even knock. She's wearing a long red coat and heels, and her hair is down and wavy. She steps inside without a word and pushes the door back until it locks with a click.

Then she removes her coat, letting it fall to the floor.

My brows rise.

Underneath she's wearing the sexiest lingerie I've ever seen—a red lace bra, which is all see-through besides a flower covering each nipple, and the matching lace panties, which connect to garters around her thighs. With the blonde hair billowing around her, and her blue eyes lined and smoky, she looks like she just stepped out of the pages of a magazine.

Nothing else comes out for a few moments while I admire her.

"Fucking hell," I whisper.

Yeah, I'm *so* glad that she decided to come back tonight. Fuck whatever else, this is the best idea we've ever had.

"Come here," I demand, and she walks over to me confidently, hips swaying. "Do you know how fucking sexy you look right now?"

Her lip twitches, and she places her hand on my chest. "I didn't until I saw the look on your face."

I pull her into me, fingers roaming down her bare back, and over the globes of her lace-covered ass. She's something else. I can't explain it.

I lift her up and she wraps her legs around me like they belong there. We kiss as I carry her back to my bed. I sit her on the bed and go down on my knees, kissing her lips, her neck, and then push her back down while I tease her inner thighs, dragging it out and enjoying the little sounds of pleasure escaping her. Then I slide her panties aside and go down on her, tasting her sweet pussy until she is crying out.

Yeah, I'm going to prove to her that tonight was a fucking good idea, too.

Spooning her, I fuck her slow and deep, and I'm so close to coming but I want to draw it out. So I roll her over, lift her hips up and lick her pussy from behind, never getting tired of her taste. I get even harder, if that's possible as she starts to get louder, her second orgasm creeping up on her. I let my tongue roam up a little and she pushes back against me, telling me she likes it.

Good girl.

She comes again, and then I slide into her and fuck her hard until I join her.

Yeah, it was the best fucking idea we've ever had.

Chapter Ten

Julianna

I didn't think he could top the first night we spent to-gether, but it's clear that Romeo is an overachiever.

And now I know firsthand how he got that nickname.

I've never done anything like this. Hell, I didn't even own any nice lingerie. I had to go out and buy some-thing new. But the look on his face right now makes it all worth it.

"You look so sexy," he says in a low, husky tone, tak-ing me in slowly from head to toe. Appreciating every inch of me. I've never felt so seen.

He circles around me, running his finger across my hip, sending shivers up my spine. The look in those brown eyes has me trembling. He gets down on his knees in front of me and pulls down my panties slowly, then kisses up my thighs until he reaches my sex.

And then he blows my whole fucking world.

The next morning Romeo rolls over and we both look into each other's eyes. His are a warm, dark brown, and up close I can see amber specks in them.

Brown eyes are now my favorite.

He just makes me feel very comfortable in my own skin. Sexy and confident. No one ever made me feel that way. As the heir to the Angels, I've been treated with kid gloves. Delicate and demure. Always the cute little girl in pigtails growing up, and as I got older, the smart, nerdy girl.

But this man. Romeo. He sees me.

Don't get it twisted, I'm not dumb enough to think this is something other than what it is, which is something casual. But he sees me as just a woman. I am simply a woman he thinks is sexy. And I've never had that. So I'm damned sure I'm going to soak this up while I can. 'Cause Lord knows Victor won't be looking at me this way. The thought of even having sex with him makes me roll my eyes.

I wouldn't have had the confidence to show up here like this for anyone else. Romeo makes me feel so beautiful and so wanted, even if I know it's only in a sexual way. I wanted a little taste of passion, and boy, did I get it.

"I had fun last night," I say, and he smiles, showing off his perfect white teeth.

"Me, too. I'm glad you came over," he murmurs, scanning my face. "Can I make you some breakfast, or do you have to run home before anyone realizes you're missing?"

If anyone goes to my house looking for me, I can just say I was at Bella's, or out for my morning run, which isn't unusual for me.

"You telling me that *the* Romeo Montanna, bad boy and ladies' man, cooks?" I tease.

"Not usually, no," he admits, a little sheepishly, running a hand up my arm. "But I can. And for you, I will."

He lifts up the white duvet and sits up, just as my phone buzzes with a message.

Victor: Date night tonight? Pick you up at seven.

"Oh fuck," I whisper to myself.

"What is it?" he asks, standing next to the bed, sliding on his black silk boxer shorts.

"Nothing," I reply a little too quickly.

He simply stares at me and arches his brow. "You sure?"

"Just…my life," I reply, hopping out of bed and realizing that I didn't actually bring any proper clothes to wear home. Just fucking great.

Romeo laughs and gets me a T-shirt out of his drawer. "Here, put this on."

"Thanks," I say, taking it from him and sliding it over my body.

He gives me a once-over and makes an "Mmm" noise. "You look good in anything, you know that?"

I smile and close the space between us. "You are pretty sweet, you know that?"

"I don't know what you're talking about," he replies, tucking my hair back behind my ear. "Now, are you going to tell me what made your face drop like it was the end of the world?"

I purse my lips. "Are we talking to each other about club shit now? Because if so, that's going to make things even messier than they already are."

He nods slowly. "Okay. Come on, then, let's eat."

I sit at the breakfast table while he makes pancakes, bacon and eggs, hip-hop music playing in the background. I've heard so much about the man in front of me.

That he's an asshole, that he's aggressive and cunning. He might be all of those things, but he's also obviously got other sides to him. He shakes his booty, doing a little dance to the beat, and I shake my head and laugh at him.

"You got a little rhythm there," I say, leaning forward on the counter. "You are full of surprises, Romeo."

He turns around and places a plate of delicious food in front of me, and one for him. "I'm a man of many talents. You can call me Johnny, you know."

This surprises me. "I thought you go by Romeo?"

He turns to me and shrugs. "I do, but it's just a nickname. My name *is* Johnny."

"I can see that," I murmur, surprised by this man in front of me. This is the man I was told is my mortal enemy. Yet I don't find anything negative about him. I pick up my fork and take a bite of the scrambled eggs. It's good, like really good.

I smile over at him. "It's delicious, thank you. Johnny."

He grins wide. "You're welcome," he says, taking a bite of his own eggs.

"So is there anything that you're not good at?" I ask, wanting to humble him just a little.

He considers my words. "Nothing I can think of."

"Of course not," I mutter, shaking my head. "How about cleaning?" I look around. "You have a cleaner here, don't you?"

"I do, but not because I can't clean. It's because a lot of the time I'm not here. So she comes in and keeps everything fresh for me. I'm actually kind of a neat freak, and I like things all kept where they are meant to be."

"Are you smart academically? How did you do in school?" I ask, but inside I already know the answer.

"Top of my class, actually. I could have done anything with my life, but my heart was always set on being a mechanic and being in the club, so that's what I did," he replies, grinning. I notice one little dimple pop up on the right side of his cheek.

"Athletic?" I press.

"Very. I used to play football, and I did martial arts for years. Muay Thai, to be exact. I did a few competitions. Do you want to see my medals?" he asks, looking on the verge of laughter.

"I'll take your word for it," I reply, lip twitching. "How do you feel about kids? And animals?"

"Love them, and they love me. I'm like that cool uncle who isn't actually your uncle."

Of course he is.

I always pay attention to the people children and animals are drawn to, because I feel like they are good people. I love how he didn't even question why I'd ask him that.

"I'm going to make it my mission to find something you aren't good at," I announce, and he laughs out loud now.

"Good luck," he replies in a cocky tone. He takes a bite of his maple syrup-covered pancake. He even chews perfectly. "Are you trying to take me down a notch or something?"

"I don't think anything could do that," I reply in a dry tone.

He puts his fork and knife down and turns to me. "And how about you? I've heard all about perfect Julianna Callisto and her real estate empire. A business mogul, I believe someone said. Oh, and I also heard you were untouchable, but I guess I proved that one wrong."

I playfully slap his arm. "Excuse me. You are an

exception to my rule. You are only the second person I've ever slept with, and no one even knows about the first. So that's probably why they say that about me."

I wonder if Victor is expecting a virgin. I bet he is, even while he goes out and sleeps with whoever he wants. I'm not an idiot, I've heard the rumors about him, and he is not innocently waiting around for our marriage. He's out there having the time of his life.

I look over and find Romeo studying me, a little too closely. "And why am I the exception?"

I shrug. "I don't know, you're sexy and incredible in bed. Oh, and I can't forget that big...big..." I look down at his crotch.

His face lights up like I've never seen, a smug expression all over it. As if he doesn't know that he is extremely blessed down there. I don't need to remind him.

"...smile of yours," I finish.

He laughs, eyes shining. "You got jokes, huh?"

"You could say that," I reply.

He shakes his head in amusement.

"So..."

"So..." he repeats.

We look at each other and laugh. "There isn't much we can talk about, is there? My life is my job and my family."

And since we're meant to be enemies, those are the things we probably shouldn't discuss.

I suppose it's hard to get to know someone when you can't let them get too close.

He looks at me thoughtfully. "There's plenty to talk about. I'll start. My favorite TV show is *Friends*. I know it's old, but I can sit there and watch reruns all day. What's yours?"

We spend the next twenty minutes talking about our mutual love of *Friends*. It's the most fun I ever had talking about nothing.

We finish up breakfast and then he offers to drive me home. "We could do a drive-by and see if it's safe. I can't send you in an Uber with what you're wearing."

I put the coat over his T-shirt. "It's fine. I came here in less than this."

His jaw tenses, and my eyes narrow, noticing. Is he feeling a little protective of me? I mean, it's not ideal wearing this in the morning, and I'm clearly doing a walk of shame.

Last night when I arrived and was all done up, I kind of looked like I was going to a club. A sex club, maybe, but one nonetheless. But now I just look like I had a long night of being properly fucked.

"I'm driving," he declares, and I roll my eyes.

"Save me from overbearing men," I grumble, but if he wants to drive me, that's fine. As long as we aren't seen, anyway.

He opens the door to his BMW and waits for me to get in. Before I do, he grips me around the waist and leans down to kiss me. It's a sweet kiss, and I don't know what it means. A goodbye, maybe.

I mean, that would be the smart thing for us. This will be the last time. First time was to get it out of our system. Second was to see if the first time was actually real. Spoiler: it was real.

When he pulls back, I'm breathless and he looks a little sad for a moment, before his expression turns guarded.

The drive home is quiet, and kind of tense, but he has

his hand on my thigh the entire time, and I like it a little too much.

"Turn left here," I say, telling him the directions until we stop in front of my house. "Looks safe."

I open my garage door for him to park in there, so we can have a moment to ourselves before he leaves. As the garage door closes, darkness locking us in, the tension builds between us. He reaches out to stroke my thigh, and unable to stop myself, I turn to him and all but jump on his lap, straddling him. He cups my face and kisses me deeply, and I reach between us, trying to get his pants off so I can have him inside me. He helps me pull his jeans down and I lift up his T-shirt and remove my panties and slide down on him, both of us gasping from the contact.

We wore a condom the first night, but kind of stopped after that, and even though I'm on the pill I know how stupid that is, because he's probably sleeping with lots of women. He's Romeo fucking Montanna, after all. They say men usually only think with their other brain, but in this situation it appears I'm just as bad, because I've been just as irresponsible.

But fuck.

I can't think straight, especially not now with his big, rock-hard cock inside of me, and his hands holding me possessively.

Right now, in this moment, this is all that matters.

He stops to pull off the coat and my top, and I moan loudly at the first contact of his tongue on my nipples. My whole body is tingling and I've never felt so alive.

I continue riding him up and down, from tip to base, lifting my hips, our lips never losing contact with each other.

And this time when we come, it's together.

Chapter Eleven

Romeo

As the garage closes shut, I get the fuck out of there before anyone sees me, speeding to the clubhouse, my body still trembling from another one of the best orgasms I've ever had. My car still smells like vanilla and sex, and my mind and body are still thoroughly fucked from our time together.

When I get to the clubhouse, I have a shower and get ready for the day. As soon as I step out of my room, my dad is there waiting for me.

"We are going out on a run tonight," he says, studying me. "Is everything okay with you? You seem distracted lately."

Fuck. "I'm fine," I reply, resting my hand against the doorframe. "And whatever you need, I'm there."

He nods slowly. "Okay. We'll leave here around seven. And Romeo?"

"Yeah?"

"You'll be taking over soon. I need you to stay focused."

Everyone keeps saying this to me. I know what is waiting for me. I don't have to be fucking reminded of it every day. Also, what the hell does it matter? What do they expect me to do? Follow my father around like a puppy? This whole "Romeo, you're taking over" shtick is getting real old. It's not like my dad is dying. He will still be around to help and guide me if I need it.

He walks away, and I rub the back of my neck, wondering how I'm going to get through the next few days. It doesn't help that I can't stop thinking about Julianna, when I have more important things to worry about.

I'm going to have to say goodbye to her, but unfortunately for us both, I'm not ready to do that just yet.

The interrogation isn't over yet, because the next person I run into in the hallway is River. We haven't spoken since that night I left him at the bar with Bella.

He nods toward the empty kitchen, and I follow him. I lean back against the countertop with my arms crossed while we have a silent conversation.

Where the fuck have you been? What happened that night with Julianna? Are you fucking crazy?

My eyes reply with: *Hey, you left with her cousin. As if you can talk.*

Her cousin is not the Princess Callisto, and I'm not about to be president. It's different and you know it.

I wince and stretch my neck from side to side. *You better not say a fucking word.*

His lips tighten. *You know that I won't, but what the fuck are you doing? Tell me it was a one-night stand.*

I look away, which gives him his answer.

"I hope you know what you are doing," he says out loud finally. "That's all I have to say. Don't get me wrong, she's fucking hot, but you are asking for trouble. You could lose everything if your dad finds out."

He's not wrong, but I am my dad's only heir. Who

else is he going to let run the club? A Montanna family member has always been president, and he's a man who hates to break tradition. Besides, no one is going to find out about Julianna. And so what if they do? I'm not the first and I won't be the last to sleep around with the Callisto women. It's not like I'm going to marry her.

"I've got it under control," I tell him, slapping him on the shoulder. "And what happened with Bella?"

He smiles a little and shrugs. "Nothing that night. I was a gentleman, unlike some people I know. But I'm taking her out on a date. She's honestly beautiful—how could I not?"

"What a fucking pair we are," I mutter to myself, and River smirks.

"Like you said, it's all under control." He doesn't even sound sure himself. I know he wouldn't say anything, because he's loyal to me over anyone, but I also know that he isn't going to approve if I continue to see Julianna.

And I get it.

It's a fucking mess.

It's also not fair that the heat would never be on River and Bella, because they aren't going to be leading their MCs. It's different for Julianna and me, and the responsibility honestly sucks.

"I heard we're going on a run tonight?" he continues, and I appreciate the subject change.

I nod. "Yeah, but I wasn't given any more details."

What's the bet they want to throw me into a situation to see if I can handle it? I know my father well. A little too well. So I need to be prepared for anything tonight, and be on top of my game.

"Should be interesting, then," he says, amusement

dancing in his eyes. "As long as no one finds out what you've been up to."

"They won't."

At least I hope not.

Well, safe to say I was right.

I was brought here to be thrown into deep water and to see if I swim or drown.

"We are separate chapters with separate business ventures—why do you think we should share our income?" my dad asks, turning to me. We're sitting around a bonfire, the members drinking with us. Casual enough setting, right? But if things go wrong, it's going to get messy. "Romeo, what do you think?"

While there are other chapters of the Devils MC and we support each other and treat each other like family, we are run by different presidents and our businesses are not the same. We have our own shit in our own city and they have theirs, unless we're working on a joint deal, which we haven't done since we stopped running drugs and guns back in the day.

Dad sits back with a beer and watches me. He could have easily spoken to me about this before we got here, but he obviously wanted to put me on the spot.

I turn to their president, Butch. "Why don't you open your own burlesque club here? I know you have the bowling alley and the smoke shop, but if that isn't making any money, time to make some changes. If you need some start-up money, we can help you with that. We want all of us to do well."

Butch nods slowly, running his fingers over his salt-and-pepper goatee. "We haven't been making much recently, and it's making it a little tense around here. I know your debt tax ends soon, so we aren't sure where you guys are at, but I think you're doing better than us by the looks of it. And in return, when shit goes south with the Angels, you know we have your back."

Yes, we will lose money from the debt tax soon enough, but we are still thriving. I can see how their chapter not having a lot coming in would cause some animosity. We have plenty of money, and if it helps them generate more income, then they won't need help again, so it's an investment.

"We will help," I assure him. "Come up with a plan and let me know."

Butch nods again as one of his men steps forward and points his finger at me. "We don't need your charity. We just want what everyone else is getting. We see your expensive bikes, houses. We're Devils, too!"

My cousin Jeremiah steps up to the man and says, "I'd calm down if I were you."

"What are you going to do about it?" he snarls, pushing Jeremiah backward. All the surrounding men stop what they are doing and look at us, getting ready to fight if they need to.

"Control your man," I demand of Butch. "Or this is about to turn ugly."

They ask for my help and then be disrespectful? I don't understand these men. This is why they don't make money—they aren't businessmen.

"Stand down," Butch commands, leading the angry biker away.

Fuck.

What next?

Twenty minutes later, Butch returns and he wants to

talk burlesque clubs. At least he has some sense. And by the end of the night, we come to an understanding.

"You handled that pretty well." Jeremiah smirks, sliding his leather gloves back on his hands.

"Thanks for having my back," I say, slapping him on the back.

"What's family for?" he says in a dry tone, getting on his bike. I would say that Jeremiah has been the black sheep of our family. With his green eyes and light hair, people have questioned his legitimacy as a Montanna. I don't think people realize how genetics work.

He's loyal, and pretty hilarious, and it hits me that I should spend more time with him. He'd be a good man to have at my side when shit goes south.

He rides off, and my dad comes over to me. "She's a lovely woman," he says.

I turn around and see him nodding toward Butch's daughter, Rachel. A cute, but kind of nerdy-looking girl I'd seen shyly avoiding people for the entirety of our visit.

"I don't need an old lady," I tell him, frowning.

I'm just about to become president, I really don't need to commit to a woman right now, especially not one he picks out. I know that Julianna will have her future husband picked by her father, and there were whispers of that person being his right-hand man, Victor. As if he would know what to do with a woman like Julianna anyway. Man is so far up her father's ass, he wouldn't have time for much else.

"Not right now you don't, but soon enough," Dad states casually, and I bury my anger at his offhand comment. He is not choosing who I take as an old lady; I will marry whoever the fuck I want to marry. No one will have control over me in that way.

There is a reason my father and I never really get along, and that's because we are both extremely stubborn. I wonder where I got it from. Shit, I don't really get along with my mother either. Grandpa Johnny and my aunt Lisa are the only two people who treat me like family. My grandmother Cathy is okay—she's a bit harsh, but at least she's fair.

My mother? Don't even get me started on my mother. She loves being an old lady and the president's wife, but she never was a mother to me. Aunt Lisa raised me. It's ironic because my mother and Aunt Lisa are sisters. Yes, two sisters married two brothers. But since Aunt Lisa had River and then Matthew and Corey, my mother just threw me to her to take care of while Mom played the role of old lady. My father may have chosen his wife, but I don't think he chose well. And I know that is not great to say about my mother, but it's the truth.

The thought of Julianna having to marry someone she doesn't want to suddenly makes me even more agitated, and I put my helmet on and speed out without another word.

As I ride home, I have a moment of clarity, a moment where I realize just how out of control I am of my own life.

And it makes me question everything.

Chapter Twelve

Julianna

"You look beautiful tonight," Victor says, not even look-ing at me.

"Thank you," I reply, laying the napkin out on my lap and glancing around the fancy restaurant. I know most people would assume I like places like this, espe-cially with all the money we make and the fact that I do enjoy some luxurious items, especially handbags and shoes, but to be honest, I'd be happier at somewhere a little low-key, or trying a new type of cuisine. Instead I'm looking at the menu and inwardly sighing, and the fact that these portions are going to leave me hungry means I'm likely going to stop at a drive-through on the way home.

But this is our first date, and I promised Dad I'd give this a chance. The second Victor picked me up, however, I knew that there will never be anything there. His eyes were empty when they looked at me, and my skin crawled when he took my hand. The car ride was mostly awk-wardly silent, and when we did speak the conversation was stiff and uncomfortable. I'm going to assume that dinner will be the same.

We both take an excruciatingly long time reading the menu, even though there are only a few options laid out before us, and I clear my throat as I place it down.

"Have you been here before?" I ask, trying to make conversation. The point of tonight was to try to get to know each other. Maybe find some common ground. We might not be physically attracted to each other, but maybe we have something in mutual interests. Do we like the same food? Music? I'm grasping at straws here, but it's desperate times. It's obvious that attraction does make all the difference, because I'm happy to talk to Romeo about any damn thing.

He nods. "Yes, I come here a lot actually. They have the best food and service in the city. Your father comes here too, so I'm surprised he hasn't taken you."

He hasn't because he knows me.

We both go quiet after that, and when the waitress arrives, I'm thankful.

"Can I get you both something to drink?" she asks, smiling kindly.

"I'll have a glass of Merlot, please," I answer, then look at Victor, who orders a whiskey on the rocks. She leaves to get our drinks and we're once again left alone with each other.

"This is nice, don't you think?" he straight out lies, and he even forces a smile. "Crazy to think that soon we will be husband and wife, and I'll be the president of the club with you at my side."

Crazy indeed.

I blink slowly. "And how do you see that going? Do you think we are compatible?"

It's time to have a real conversation. The small talk isn't going to get us anywhere. And if I'm being honest, I want him to admit that he agrees with me, that this whole thing is a terrible idea. Surely he has some concerns about this. He can't blindly just want to marry a woman he has no connection with.

"It doesn't matter, Julianna" is his sharp reply. His brows furrow at my comment. "This is the way that things are going to be. And I think we should try to make the most of it."

Maybe he does just blindly want to marry me, then. But not to *be* with me.

He wants me for the position it gives him.

"And what kind of marriage are we going to have?" I ask, pursing my lips. "Are you going to be faithful to me?"

He leans back in his seat and studies me. For a second there, I feel like he's going to finally give me some honesty, but then he must change his mind. "Is that what you require of me?"

We're going around in fucking circles.

"Is there no other woman you love or are interested in? I know you haven't been celibate all of this time," I say quietly, so only he can hear.

He grits his teeth. "I know you don't want this marriage, Julianna, but this is how it's going to be. Everything before this doesn't matter. I will be a good husband to you. And an even better president."

Fucking hell.

He wants to be president more than anything, and he will clearly do anything to make that happen. I'm just one of the pawns on the chessboard. And he's not going to try to see it from my perspective. He doesn't care about me at all.

"And what do you expect from me?" I ask.

"I expect you to act appropriately, and to not embarrass me. To run and organize the club events, to look after me and the men. To keep making money for the club with your real estate knowledge. And to always show me respect. You've seen the role your mother has played and you should know to do the same."

My mother is the perfect stay-at-home wife, so he wants me to do that, but also to make the money. Basically just shut up and listen to him.

Does he think his dick is made of gold?

"And children?" I ask. This is the most he's said to me in all I've known him.

"You will bear me as many children as necessary to produce a boy."

What the ever-loving fuck? I grip the napkin in my lap tightly.

"I'm sorry. You want me to keep having children until I have a boy?" I must've heard him wrong. "You do know how biology works, right? Your sperm determines the sex of the baby. It has nothing to do with me."

He rolls his eyes. "I know that, but I will end this Callisto reign of women."

"And do I have a say in this?" I'm supposed to have sex with this man? You've got to be kidding.

"No. As my wife, your wifely duty will be to produce an heir."

"Having a girl is producing an heir."

"No it is not. It is having a child to marry off. I want an heir."

I fucking hate him.

Ever since I was a little girl, I've wanted to run the MC. Not just in the kitchen baking, but I've wanted to run it side by side with my husband, making decisions and money together.

This is my legacy, and it means something to me.

Victor wasn't born into this. I was.

Success isn't sexually transmittable, but for him, being with me gives him all that he needs.

"I'm a smart woman, and I have ideas for the club that would generate even more income and could stop a war from starting with the Devils—"

"You don't have a say in things like war, Julianna. You are a woman, you should know your place."

I'm not going to lie, I have to physically stop myself from reaching over the table and knocking him out. "Nice to know where your head is at, Victor," I mutter.

Our drinks arrive and I swallow mine in two gulps. I have to figure a way out of this that doesn't involve murder. That's my last resort. I'm only halfway kidding. We order our meals, and when Victor goes to the bathroom I quickly check my phone.

Johnny: Coming over tonight?

Julianna: Yes. Give me about two hours.

Johnny: Okay. But I have to leave by midnight. Where are you?

Julianna: Hell.

Johnny: Are you okay??

Julianna: I'm fine.

No point telling him I'm on a date with my future husband. I know we are going to have to have these conversations soon, that or we stop seeing each other, but right now doesn't seem like the time.

Johnny: I can come and get you.

Shit.

Julianna: I'm fine, I promise. I'm out at dinner.

Johnny: With who?

Victor returns and I put my phone back in my handbag. The dead conversation commences. The food turns out to be pretty good, but I was right about the portions, and I end up getting McDonald's before heading to Romeo's.

Dinner with my future husband.

Then to my lover's house for a night of hot sex.

What a fucking life I live.

When he opens the door, I hand him the Oreo McFlurry I got him. "I brought you dessert."

He flashes me a grin and pulls me against him with a hand on my hip. "Thank you. I didn't know they had ice cream in hell."

"Not in, just on the way home," I reply, closing the door behind me. I know he's nosy about where I was tonight, but I can't be angry. If the situation was reversed, I'd feel the same. "I was out having dinner, like I told you. It wasn't fun. Now I'm here to make my night a little more exciting."

He studies me and licks the ice cream off his spoon. "And who were you having dinner with?"

I head to his bedroom and he stalks behind me. Like I said to him before, once we delve into these conversations, things will start to get even more complicated than they are. Romeo doesn't need to know too much about what goes on in our club, because at any stage that could come to bite me in the ass. But at the same time, how do we not discuss certain things? The closer we get, the harder it will be to not tell each other everything.

Once we cross this line, I feel like there's no going back.

I answer him, or I walk away.

As we reach his bedroom, he grabs my wrist and I spin around and look at him in the eye.

He puts the ice cream down on the bedside table and stands closely in front of me, his beautiful brown eyes peering into my soul. "Who were you having dinner with? Don't make me ask again."

Fuck.

"Victor," I reply.

His eyebrows rise and then furrow as he figures it all out. "So the rumors are true—they want you to marry him."

I nod slowly.

"When?" he asks, fingers tightening before letting my arm go.

"Soon. I've managed to put it off for a while as long as I go out with him and try to get to know him. Hence the dinner. And before you ask, no, I don't want to marry him. He's older than me, and we have no chemistry at all. He's ambitious, though, and really wants this," I explain.

"Interesting," Romeo mutters, then cups my face. "What a fucked-up situation we're in."

"You have no idea," I whisper.

His lips press against mine gently. "Right now you're mine, and that's all that matters."

In a second we're all over each other, clothes getting ripped off, both of us on the bed, him on top of me. There's almost a desperation in our sex, as if we both know that what he said isn't true.

Not that I'm his right now.

But that it's all that matters.

Eventually, we're going to have to face the music, but not tonight.

Tonight is ours.

Chapter Thirteen

Romeo

I eat ice cream sitting up in bed with Julianna, both of us still naked, our bare legs sprawled over the black silk sheets. She just finished filling me in on her latest "date" with her fiancé. Prick.

I don't like hearing about Victor. The thought of her spending time with him kills me, never mind the fact that she's going to have to marry him. What started as a one-time thing turned into a...quasi-relationship? We see each other almost every day, even if it's a quick thirty-minute meal outside of town. We know we're playing with fire and that there is an end date for whatever this is. But fuck, we're enjoying what we're doing.

And now I know I messed up. I should have stayed away from her from the beginning. Things would have been a lot simpler, but now it's hard to imagine letting her go. I glance over at her to find her already looking at me, a gentleness in her eyes, and I wonder if she's thinking the same thing as me.

"I don't know what we're going to do, but it's going to be okay," I say, leaning down to kiss her on the forehead. I'm not sure why I'm making promises I can't keep, or why I'm even making them. All I know is that I don't want her to have to worry.

"I don't want to marry him," she whispers, and I close my eyes as I hear the words. She shouldn't have to marry anyone she doesn't want to. It's modern times now, but our families still live in the past, filled with traditions that they stick to like they are law. No one has ever broken the Montanna and Callisto traditions. Something makes me feel like Julianna and I may be the first.

"We'll find a way so you don't have to," I find myself saying.

I don't know how, but I'd do anything to be able to give her whatever she wants. How would I be a man if I sat around and turned my head the other way? I care about her. I love spending my nights with her. I don't want her to be with any other man. I'm not sure how the fuck we got here, but she's gotten under my skin, and I'm not going to allow her to just get married off like a piece of property. I don't remember when I got so fucking righteous, but apparently she does that to me.

Choosing Julianna means that I'm putting my own position with my club at risk, and I need to think about this rationally.

Am I doing the right thing, or am I just thinking with my dick?

I can't throw everything away.

"I want to be with you," she finally says. We've been skirting this issue for some time. I guess now's as good a time as ever to be honest.

I put the ice cream on the bedside table and grab her hand in mine. "I want to be with you, too. I can't imagine you marrying Victor, or anyone else but me."

Her eyes go wide. "Are you...did you...are we... What are you saying?"

Shit.

Okay, I think we are doing this. "I think I just proposed to you."

I don't want to live my life without her in it. I know how crazy it sounds because we haven't known each other that long. But when you know, you know.

I'm screwed. We're going to have to move to fucking Mexico or something, and change our names. We might have to give it all up, but this somehow seems the easier option, because leaving her isn't going to happen.

There is another option, and it's fucking wild, but we could join the two MCs and lead them together. I don't know how we'd make that work, but it's the only way we can keep each other and our family legacies together.

She stays quiet for a few moments after that, but wraps her arm around me and squeezes tightly. "Well, then I'm saying yes," she finally says.

As happy of a moment as this is, we don't say a word and stay wrapped in each other all night.

So much happened, and I don't know if I spoke without thinking, or if I'm for once just following my heart.

When the sun rises, she heads back home and I wonder how long we're going to be able to pull this off before it catches up with us.

I have a fiancée I can't talk to anyone about. I want to marry a Callisto when my family hates them.

And this is one love grudge that will never be let go.

I'm distracted when I head to the clubhouse, and River notices it right away. We're both sitting outside, drinks in hand, enjoying a peaceful moment.

"What's going on with you?" he asks, even though he knows the answer. She's about five foot six with beautiful blonde hair and smells like vanilla.

"Nothing," I reply, stretching my neck from side to side. "Church tonight."

When the president calls for a club meeting, he calls it church. And the fact that we're all meeting has me on edge. Is my dad finally going to step down tonight? He's been dangling it over my head for months. And what about Julianna?

When did my life get so fucking messy?

River nods and slaps me on the back. "You were born for this, Romeo. This is the moment we've been waiting for."

"I know."

But my priorities have changed. I want the Devils MC *and* Julianna.

I just need to figure out a way to do that without sacrificing one of them.

River, unaware of the war going on in my head, continues talking. "Do you think it will be tonight?"

"I don't know," I admit, taking a sip of my beer. "He did say it will be soon, but you never know with him. He's been saying that for months."

Once I'm president, I'll be all in with the club, and I won't have as much free time as I do now. I won't be able to see Julianna every night, but if she needed me, I'd be there. Day or night, I'd have to make it work.

Matthew comes out, grabs a beer from the bar fridge and sits down on the other side of me. "What have I missed?"

"Don't know yet, but we'll find out at church tonight," I say, raising my glass bottle to his. We clink.

"Change is coming," he states, swallowing a gulp. "And it starts with you."

His words hit me right in the gut, because I feel the same way.

Change *is* coming.

But are they ready for the change I'm going to make?

The rest of the MC show up, and we all play pool and talk shit. It reminds me that I grew up with these men and I love them all—I need to show up for them. I need to be there for them and look out for their best interests.

My phone buzzes with a text from Julianna, and I step into the kitchen to read it, even though she's just saved in my phone as a J.

J: I miss you.

Romeo: Miss you too. I'm playing pool at the club-house. What are you up to?

J: V wants to go for a walk on the beach.

Motherfucker. I hope he keeps his hands to himself.

Romeo: He better behave. He'll be with my fiancée, after all.

J: Are we really doing this?

Romeo: I meant it when I asked. Did you mean it when you said yes?

The three dots come up then disappear. Appear. Disappear.

J: I meant it. We just need to figure out how to deal with V and my father.

Romeo: Want me to come drown Victor?

  I'm only half joking.

J: No. Not yet anyway. I'll be fine. And thinking of you the whole time.

Romeo: We have church, and I might not be able to see you tonight, depending on how it goes.

J: They're going to make you president?

Romeo: I don't know yet.

J: That's huge.

  Before I can reply she sends another message.

J: Does it change anything?

  If that isn't the question of the day.

Romeo: I'm going to make it work. We will make it work.

  "Why you hiding back here?" River asks, lighting up a smoke. "Afraid you're going to get your ass kicked in pool again?"
  If only that were my biggest fear right now.
  I've been hearing a rumor going around that I really

need to speak to Julianna about, and I'm not looking forward to it.

"When was the last time that happened? Must have been so long ago I can't even remember," I reply in a dry tone.

And then my dad arrives and shit gets real.

Chapter Fourteen

Julianna

I'm walking along the beach with Victor, in our usual uncomfortable silence, but all I can think about is the fact that the next time I see Romeo he could be president of the Devils MC.

Our sworn enemy.

And the man I'm engaged to. The man I love.

"I have some new ideas on how to run the club," Victor says. When he does speak it's about the MC, never about us as a couple. Nor does he ever try to get to know me. I'm a means to an end, and that's it, and I'm not even allowed to question it. A foregone conclusion.

"There will be some changes happening soon, and, of course, you will be helping with the real estate side of things and bringing more income in for us."

"I'll be helping with more than just the real estate," I reply, stopping in my tracks.

He turns and faces me. "I'll be president, Julianna. And at the end of the day you are still just an old lady."

Wow.

"That might be so, but without me you wouldn't be

president at all," I fire back. "It is my birthright that my husband be president. You are replaceable, I am not."

Yeah, he doesn't like that. His face gets red and I can almost see smoke come out of his ears. "Doesn't matter how I get there, I am still going to be president, and you are still just a woman. You have your place and I have mine. Your father chose me because of my ability to lead, among other things," he replies, jaw tight.

He's angry but trying to control it. When I'm his wife, will he still try to hold himself back? I think not.

"I've also been raised to lead," I tell him, crossing my arms over my chest. "I'm not a meek little girl, Victor. And I understand we have our roles, but I will be seen and treated as an equal."

"We aren't equals," he says, looking back at me in disbelief. "I am a man, you are a woman. What is there to understand? I always thought that your father was too lenient with you."

I arch my brow. He is such a sexist, controlling asshole. "Maybe this getting-to-know-each-other thing was a bad idea."

Because now I know for sure what a selfish prick he is.

"I thought so too, but your father insisted. Like I said, he likes to humor you. I have no idea why," he grumbles, as he starts to walk again.

I storm after him. "Maybe because he knows the value that I bring to the clubhouse. I've almost doubled the MC income in the last few years. We are making bank, and legally, because of me."

"Yes, and I have told you that you handle the real estate business and keep doing what you've been doing. But the actual MC, and the men who belong to it, will be led by me, and I will make decisions to keep the club thriving. You worry about the numbers, and I'll worry about everything else."

"So I will have no say in anything else?"

"You can just look pretty and do what you want to do, but club business is my own."

I'm angry at his words, but I hide that fact.

This club is my family.

My legacy.

My traditions.

He is so easily replaceable, and I wonder if he knows that.

We walk in silence back to the parking lot, where I thankfully arrived in my own car. Probably because I knew I'd want to make an escape.

I get into my car without a word, and he waits until I'm inside before he does the same. I'd think it chivalrous, but let's be real, of course he wouldn't want anything to happen to his property. He needs me for his plans to play out, willing or not.

On my drive home, I realize I need to start taking action. I want to marry Romeo and not Victor. If I keep letting this charade go on, I'll be closer to having to marry Victor.

I hope that Romeo can see me tonight, but if he was sworn in he'll likely have to stay at the clubhouse. His life is about to change, and I'm happy for him, but I don't know where I'm going to fit into it. Sure, he proposed and I said yes. But what does that mean? We have too much at stake and too many people against this.

I know it would be for the best for us to walk away from each other now. But deep inside I hope that he doesn't do that. He's the only thing getting me through these days. I send him a text as soon as I get home.

Julianna: You awake?

Johnny: Yeah.

Julianna: Can you come over?

Johnny: Now?

Shit.

Julianna: Yeah.

Johnny: Yeah okay, I'll text you when I'm there so you can open the garage.

The last thing I need is for anyone to see his car parked out front of my place. I have a shower and get dressed into my pink silk pajamas.

Johnny: I'm here.

I hit the button to open the garage door and watch as his car is revealed. He parks it and I close the door behind him. When he gets out of the car, I see the president patch on his cut. I'm not going to lie, it looks sexy as fuck on him. I don't know what it is about powerful men, or maybe it's just him, but I want to rip all of his clothes off.

"Congratulations," I say, reaching out and touching the patch. "It looks good on you."

"Thanks," he replies, smiling, his eyes roaming over my body. "You look cute as fuck right now."

"Thanks," I say with a grin, and then take his hand and lead him back to my room. "I'm glad that you're here."

"Me too, sorry it's so late. We were celebrating at the clubhouse," he says, pulling off his clothes as he steps into my bedroom. This is the first time he's been in here, and I wait as he looks around.

"This is exactly the kind of room I would have pictured you in," he says, amusement in his tone.

I glance around my all-white bedroom, wondering what he means. "How so?"

"It's perfect, not an item out of place, fancy as fuck, yet somehow warm."

His shirt comes off and I get distracted by his hard, smooth chest and ripped abs. "It's just a room."

"I haven't been in your bed yet," he notes, undoing his belt with his eyes locked on me.

"I haven't been with a president yet," I tease, sitting back on the bed and watching the show. Shoes and jeans come off and then he's in all his naked glory right in front of me, hard cock pointing at me like an arrow.

I take him in my hand and stroke, before tasting him, my tongue licking the head of him before sucking in as much as I can, just how he likes it.

He threads his hands in my hair while I work my magic, his moans encouraging me and turning me on even more.

I'm wet, and he hasn't even touched me.

He has that effect on me.

I want him to come in my mouth now, but he doesn't allow that. Instead he gets down on his own knees, removes my baggy pajamas and goes down on me until I scream his name. Then he fucks me from behind, slow and deep, until we both finish together.

As we lie next to each other, only our feet touching as we catch our breaths, the truth of the situation hits me.

I am not willing to let go of Johnny Montanna.

I'm following in my grandmother's footsteps, except I want the happily-ever-after.

But what a fight it's going to be.

Chapter Fifteen

Romeo

I probably shouldn't have come here tonight, and I hadn't intended on it. But after a few celebration drinks with the Devils, the only person I wanted was her, and when she texted me, I took the chance to drive over here. Not the best idea, but I can't regret it. I can't regret any time spent with her, no matter how risky.

I'm still processing the whole president thing. When we went into church and my dad looked at me, I knew he was handing over the reins. He took off his president patch and gave it to me, and I have to admit I felt a little guilty considering he doesn't know anything about me and Julianna.

But at the same time I do feel deserving of the title. I was born to be president, and now at the young age of twenty-eight I know I'll be a damn good one. I'll be expected to live at the clubhouse now, as is tradition, so getting away is going to be harder to explain, but I'll think of something. As my grandfather says, if there is a will, there is a way. Although I never thought I would apply that to sleeping with a Callisto, but here we are.

When the sunshine creeps through her cream curtains in the morning, I think I know a solution to our problem. We've been tiptoeing around this and all we do is talk about it. It's time we take action.

I run my fingers down her bare back and wonder what our life would be like if we were like any other normal couple. We could spend the day together and not have a care in the world about who saw us. Things that other people take for granted.

I kiss her shoulder and she makes an "Mmm" noise but doesn't stir, so I slide out of bed, use her bathroom and then turn on her coffee machine. Her house is beautiful, elegant and modern, with no expense spared. I put two mugs on the black marble counter and am searching for sugar when I hear a knock at the door.

Fuck. I rush back into her bedroom.

"Julianna," I whisper, gently shaking her. "Someone is at the door."

She lifts her head, eyes widening. She looks so beautiful, even first thing in the morning. "What? What time is it?"

"Six."

Sitting up, she slides her robe on and turns to me. "You stay here."

"Call out if you need me," I tell her, even though I doubt she will—not like a burglar would be knocking on the damn door. I eye her closet and wonder if I'm going to have to hide in there if her dad or whoever steps inside the house.

Fucking hell, I feel like a teenager again.

"Rosalind, what are you doing here so early?" I hear her say loudly.

Rosalind?

This just keeps getting worse. I know they're family, but what are the odds?

I grab my clothes and shoes off the floor and get my ass in the closet, hoping she doesn't come into the room. I still haven't told Julianna about the little fact that I have slept with Rosalind before, and I also haven't told her the rumor I heard about Victor.

"I'm sorry, I didn't mean to wake you up. I was on my way to yoga and realized that I forgot my bag with my change of clothes in it—do you have something I can borrow?" Rosalind asks.

Julianna's tone is exasperated as she replies, "Can't you just go home and get your bag? We aren't even the same size."

Rosalind gasps. "Are you saying I'm fat?"

"No, that's not what I meant—"

"Do you have some activewear or something? Give me something and I'll be on my way."

Julianna sighs, and then tells her to wait at her bedroom door and she will find something. She opens the drawer next to her bed and pulls out some pants and a top. "Here. And I want these back—they're new."

"Thanks," Rosalind says, smiling. She steps into the bedroom, and Julianna tries to usher her out, but fails, with Rosalind lingering. I feel like a Peeping Tom watching and listening to their conversation through the little gap in the closet door, but there's not much else I can do right now. "I can't believe you're going to be married soon. Are you going to have a bachelorette party? I could throw you one."

"No, I don't think so," Julianna replies, confusion in her tone. I wonder how close they are. They could be as close as River, Matthew and me. That would be bad. That would be real bad. "I don't want to have any party."

"Why not?"

"I just don't," Julianna replies, shrugging. "It's not a love match, I don't feel like there's much to be celebrating."

Rosalind's eyes widen, like she's surprised by Julianna's lack of enthusiasm. "He's good-looking, and he's pretty badass. You could do worse. Dad picked him for you, so…"

Dad?

No. No way. Rosalind is *not* her sister. Please tell me that is not the situation. This is a cruel, sick world if this is true.

"Well, it doesn't matter, does it? Now, if you don't mind…"

She all but drags Rosalind out of the room and to the front door. Luckily she didn't go into the kitchen and see the two mugs and hot coffee, because that would have been a dead giveaway.

"You can come out now," she says a few minutes later. "Rosalind never drops by here; I don't know why she decided to today."

I open the closet and step out, still naked, clothes and shoes in my hands. "That was close."

I gulp. I have to come clean. I have to tell her about Rosalind and me.

"Lucky she's not very observant," she murmurs, eyes going down my body and lingering on my cock. "I'm about to have a shower—would you like to join me?"

My lip twitches.

Of course I fucking do.

But I can't. Not with this secret hanging over my head.

"I have to go. First day as president." After I'm dressed, I kiss her goodbye. "We have to make some plans. There's a lot to discuss. Tonight?"

She nods while biting her lip. I kiss her again, get in my car and speed away the second the garage door opens, before anyone else can drop in, or someone sees me.

Shit is about to get interesting.

Chapter Sixteen

Julianna

Romeo leaves and luckily no one manages to see him. I couldn't believe Rosalind dropped in here, and so early, which is so out of character for her. It makes me a little suspicious, as if she might know something. Rosalind never does anything without reason. She may come off as ditzy and emotional, but she can be very calculating.

I head to the clubhouse to finalize some contracts I left there and then go and visit my grandma. I know it's a gamble, but I think opening up to her with my problems right now might be the only answer. I find her in her bedroom at my mom's house, sitting facing the window with a coffee in her hands. She moved in here after Mikey died so she wouldn't be alone in her home, but I wonder if she misses it here.

"Nanny?" I say gently, as not to scare her. "Are you okay?"

I forget that she is still grieving, and probably misses her husband like crazy. I miss him, too. But I really should spend more time with her than I have been. I know she must be lonely.

"I'm good," she replies, smiling. "How are you, my

dear? You look well. Actually, really well—you are glow-
ing."

I can feel my face heat at her comment. "I am doing
fine. Just thought I would drop in and see how you are,
and see if you needed help with anything."

She waves her hand in the air. My grandmother is
still so beautiful even in her seventies. Her formerly
blonde hair is a beautiful silver and her blue eyes shine
with youth. "I don't need help, everything is done for
me here. I think I might go back to my own house. Me
staying here is not necessary. I'm not an invalid. I'm still
capable of doing everything and managing my home
on my own."

"If that would make you happier," I reply, sitting down
on her bed. "We thought you would like the company."

"I thought I would too," she admits, putting her glass
mug on the bedside table. "But now I just miss my home.
And the memories there."

"I understand."

"Now, what are you really here about?" she asks, getting straight to the point, which is just like her. "You
look like you have something on your mind."

"I don't want to marry Victor," I blurt out, lowering my voice in case my parents walk by. "The time is
nearing, and Dad won't listen to me."

Her blue eyes flash with sympathy. "Has Victor done
anything to you? Or you just don't want to marry him,
period? Explain to me what's going on in your head."

I shift on the bed and wring my hands as I talk. "I'm
just a means to an end for Victor. He hasn't bothered to
get to know me, he doesn't think we are equals. I don't
love him, I don't even like him! The thought of having
to marry him makes my skin crawl."

She reaches out and takes my hand, stopping my fidgeting. "And what did your father say?"

"He wouldn't listen. I managed to stall a little, by saying I would get to know him better first, much to Victor's dismay."

"Have you spoken to your mom?" she asks.

I shake my head. "She won't go against what my dad has decided. There's no point. They want me to do my duty and marry Victor so he can lead the MC. I've always known it was going to happen, but now that it's here I'm freaking out. And..."

I bite my lip. I don't know how much I should tell her, but for three months I haven't been able to talk to anyone about this. And I think we need to act sooner rather than later. I need someone on my side.

Nanny grabs my hand. "Sweet pea, did you meet someone?" she asks softly.

I start to cry and just nod.

"Oh, honey. Do you love him?"

I nod again.

"Tell me."

I take a deep breath and make a decision right there to just go for it. "I'm in love with Johnny Montanna."

My grandmother brings her hands to her mouth. Shit. Is it really that bad?

Nanny composes herself and her eyes are wild as they look at me. "Sweet pea, he's in his seventies."

What?

"I want to support you, dear, but I don't quite understand..."

Oh my God. Now I know why she is so shocked.

"No, Nanny, no. Not *that* Johnny Montanna. The younger one. Romeo."

"Oh," Nanny says, visibly relieved. But then she processes what I said. "OH! Julianna, no."

I sigh. "I know. It's bad."

"It's not bad, sweet pea. It's the worst thing that you could do."

"But I love him. You got to marry who you wanted; I just want the same opportunity. I want to marry for love, not obligation."

She purses her lips and lets go of my hand. "Actually, I didn't get to marry who I wanted. It's a long story—"

"What do you mean?" I ask, brow furrowing. "We've all heard your love story; it's legendary."

"You heard what you were meant to hear," she replies, smiling sadly. "The truth wasn't exactly that, it was a little more complicated. I know more than others how hard it is trying to navigate this family and this world, Julianna."

"Tell me?" I request. "Only if you want to, of course."

The story we were always told was that Mikey was her true love, and that she had followed her heart to be with him, even if it was frowned upon, and even if it broke Johnny's heart to do so. I imagine that for Johnny, it would have been the ultimate betrayal. Your girlfriend and your best friend?

I know that had to hurt.

But if that is not the story, then I have no idea why things played out the way they did.

She looks out the window. "I would have never spoken of this if Mikey were alive, but now he's gone so…" She's silent for a moment before she continues. "I loved Mikey, I did. He was a wonderful husband and gave me many great years."

"But?"

She ducks her head. "But before that I was head over

heels in love with Johnny Montanna. And I think I always will be. He was my first love, my soulmate. My true love."

My eyes widen. This goes against everything I was ever told. "Then why did you leave him for Mikey?"

She takes a deep breath and tucks her silver hair back behind her ear. "I loved Johnny with everything I had, and he treated me like an equal, unlike your Victor. His father hated that. He didn't approve of how much influence I had over Johnny. He never liked me. And one day Johnny's father cornered me at my house and told me that if I did not leave Johnny, he would destroy my family. I believed him. I opened up and told Mikey about it; we were both close with him, and he told me he'd help me figure it out. But Johnny's father had his men start following me. Showing up where I was. Threatening me without saying anything. Mikey finally suggested that I leave with him. He always loved me. I knew that. And eventually I learned to love him back, but my heart always belonged to Johnny. Mikey knew that, too. But he said he'd rather have a piece of me than none of me."

"I had no idea," I whisper, processing her words. "And Johnny still has no idea it was his father who pulled you away from him?"

She shakes her head. "We told no one about this. You're the first person I'm telling. I never wanted it to seem like I didn't love Mikey, because I did, but that's the truth. I let Johnny's father bully me into giving him up. Looking back, if I had been braver, or handled it differently... I don't know. I could have had a completely different life. But there's no point thinking about the what-ifs."

"He's still alive, you know. You could talk to him now. It's never too late."

She smiles, and it's the saddest one I've ever seen. "He's still married, ironically to the woman who was my best friend at the time. An eye for an eye, I suppose."

Jesus Christ.

What a mess.

"I still think he should know the truth. Life is too short for him to never know that you really did love him," I say gently, touching her hand with my own. "And thank you for sharing that with me, Nanny. I know it must be painful for you to relive it."

"I think about it every day, and have for my whole life," she admits. "I don't want you to live your life with regrets, Julianna."

She's right.

If I want to be with Johnny, my Johnny, then I'm going to have to fight for it.

I need to talk to Johnny.

I get up and kiss her on the cheek. "Thanks. I need to figure some things out. I'll be back."

I send Romeo a text telling him I want to talk to him, and when can he come back over.

Johnny: Tonight.

Tonight we will know what path we choose.
And I'm both exhilarated, and scared shitless.

Chapter Seventeen

Romeo

I'm knee-deep in shit when Julianna messages me. I reply to her, wondering what she wants to talk about and if maybe something has happened, while dealing with the men at the same time. We started going to the different bars and clubs, ending with me at Devil's Play, and River managed to get himself into a fight with one of our members, pulling his gun on him.

Trent, a guy who's about twenty years older than us, gets in River's face. "Are you always going to be Romeo's lackey? Just following his orders?"

River smirks, still pointing a gun at him. "Yes. I follow my president's orders. You know when you don't it's called treason?"

Trent is one of the men who openly opposes me being president of the Devils MC. It's always been like this—the older men don't respect the younger ones right away. And I know that how I handle him right now is going to set a precedent. With my hand on River's chest, gently pushing him back, I stare Trent down. He's in his fifties, so I get it, he might not want to get ordered by someone younger than him, or he might not be ready for change.

But that's how things are going to be, so he needs to accept it.

"I know that you're having a hard time processing all the changes going on right now, but I am your president, whether you like it or not," I tell him in a low tone. "River shouldn't have to feel like he needs to defend me from one of my own men. If you don't like it, you know where the door is. I'm not dealing with any fucking disrespect, do you hear me?"

Trent grits his teeth, his jaw tight and unwavering.

"Are you a Devil, or not?" I ask once more.

He nods slowly. "I am. I have been for twenty years now."

"Then trust that my father has done the right thing by stepping down and putting me in charge," I say, letting go of River, who lowers his weapon. "Let me show you what I'm made of. Give it some time and you will see that my age doesn't define me. My dad was the same age when he became president."

River gets closer to him. "You talk shit about him again, and no one will be able to hold me back."

Trent looks at me. I think he's about to back down when he whispers under his breath, "Teenybopper."

Before River can react, I swing back and punch Trent in the face. He goes down with one swing. The other men around him stare at me, speechless.

Trent stares at me from the ground, a look of incredulity on his face. I point a finger at him. "That will be the last time you ever show me disrespect. You got me?" I'll be damned if I let some old-timer lip off to me.

Caden, Trent's son—we are a family establishment—reaches down to give his father his hand. "Are we going to have problems?" I ask Caden.

His father stands and Caden turns to me. "No, Prez. I'm good."

"I'm good too, Prez," Trent says while rubbing the side of his face.

They both walk off without another word and I stare at the rest of the men that witnessed that.

"Anyone else have a problem?" When no one says anything, I turn around and head to the bar and River follows suit.

"Fucking mutiny already," I mutter, rubbing the back of my neck.

"We knew it was coming. They will challenge you, test you, and finally, when you're about to kill them yourself, they will respect you," he says with a grin, slapping me on the back.

I'm glad he's on my side.

But he's right, I did know this was going to happen. I just didn't know I was going to have...other things I'd be dealing with at the same time, making it a very fucking stressful combination.

I pick up my beer and before it hits my lips say, "Let the games begin."

River laughs beside me. "So when's the party? We have to celebrate your reign, invite everyone. It's been a while since we've had something big at the clubhouse."

He's right, I should be socializing right now, mingling with the families of the members and letting everyone feel comfortable and safe. Start off on the right foot. "Yeah, that's probably a good idea. This weekend?"

"I'll get the word out."

I wish I could take Julianna to things like this, show

her off. Instead I'll be on my own, pretending I'm single. It's a little fucking depressing, really.

Only I'm not single.

I'm someone who is usually always single, even if I'm casually seeing someone.

This is the first time I'm considering myself off the market in my life.

I'm Romeo Fucking Montanna.

What has she done to me?

Echo comes over, paperwork in her hands, unaware of my internal struggles. "Safe to come out now?"

"Trent hasn't been hassling you, has he?" I ask, frowning as the thought occurs.

She sits down next to me and shakes her head. "No, he's okay. I'd tell you if there were any problems."

I nod, satisfied.

"I think we might need to hire a few new people," she admits, looking over the weekly roster. "We are getting busy and need it to be flexible for the women too, so I think a couple more would help."

"Prez here can hold the auditions," River teases.

But Echo simply nods. "Actually, I think that would be good, if you were with me during the auditions and could meet the dancers. If they know they are safe here, they are likely to want the job and be happier."

"Okay, tell me when and I'll be there," I reply, wondering how Julianna is going to feel about that one. She has been raised in an MC, though, so she knows what it's like. But at the end of the day she's a woman and I'd want to rip a man apart if the roles were reversed.

Hopefully she is more civilized than me.

"Say next Thursday, one p.m.," she says, marking it

down on her little planner. "I'll make an ad and tell the girls to get the word out."

"Wonderful," I mutter. Echo doesn't walk off, though. "Is there something else?"

I can tell on her face she's debating saying something. "We've been having a lot of Angels coming in lately. They haven't been causing problems, but they've been...rowdy."

What the hell are the Angels doing? "Anyone in particular who's been rowdy?"

"Um. Victor. He gets a bit handsy with the waitresses."

Fucking Victor. He's become the bane of my existence. I turn to River. "I think we need to pay the Angels a bit of a visit. Introduce them to the new president."

River nods. "We going now?"

I take a look at my watch: six p.m. "Yeah, let's go."

We ride off into the night looking for some Angels.

We head to a bar that is known as an Angels hangout. They don't own any bars or clubs—that was off-limits when Mikey formed the Angels. We get the nightlife, and the Angels can take on whatever other businesses they want.

River and I pull up to Scotty's, a pub on the other side of town, and sure enough, we see a row of bikes lined up. Victor has to be here.

When I walk in, I scan the room and see Victor sucking face with a brunette on his lap. I turn to River and whisper in his ear, "Who's the brunette?" River is the biggest gossip. He knows everything that is going on. Half of him likes just being in the know, the other half loves the gossip like a schoolgirl.

"Veronica. Paulie's youngest daughter. Julianna and Rosalind's youngest sister."

I have so many questions after those statements. First, he knew Julianna and Rosalind were sisters? Fucker never told me. Second, the rumors of Victor and Veronica together are true. Fuck. This is a Greek tragedy waiting to happen.

I head over to Victor since he seems to be the ranking member here. There's no way he'd be openly making out with Paulie's youngest when he's betrothed to the oldest, right? But apparently this man has no shame, because that's exactly what he is doing.

"Victor," I say and everyone just stares at me. Except Victor, whose tongue is down Veronica's throat. This guy is vile.

"Victor," I say again, and rap on the table with my knuckles.

When he finally comes up for air, he glances at me in mild amusement. I think I'm going to have some fun with this fucker. I turn to Veronica, feigning ignorance.

"You must be Julianna. I heard you and Victor were to be married." I reach out a hand to shake it. River starts chuckling to himself.

The girl can't be more than twenty years old. She looks at my hand, then to Victor, who just stares at me with no emotion.

She finally takes my hand. "No, I'm Veronica." She glances at Victor one more time, then gets up before saying, "I should be going."

When she leaves, Victor and his men continue to eye me. "What are you doing here?" he finally says.

I grab a chair and pull it over. "To introduce myself. Formally. As the president of the Devils MC. Seeing as you've been venturing over to our businesses, I figured I should make it known."

Victor takes a drink. "So it's a crime to go into a bar?" His buddies chuckle.

I've had enough of his shit, I have better things to do. I stand up, the chair scratching on the floor. "No, but it's a crime to come into my club and harass my employees. Next time you'll be leaving in a body bag."

Victor laughs. "I'll be president of the Angels in no time, and when that happens, you Devils won't know what hit you. And without *our* money from the tax debt, I'm sure your pathetic excuse of an empire will soon be crumbling anyway."

I take a step forward and all of his men stand. He slowly stands too and we're eye to eye. Well, I'm eye to forehead. I have a few inches on him. "You're putting the cart before the horse. Rumor has it the princess of the Angels wants nothing to do with you."

His eye twitches and he shoves me so hard that I fall back into River. Victor points a finger at me. "Watch it, pretty boy. Your face won't be so pretty when I'm done with you."

It's my turn to laugh, and just as I turn to leave, I swing a right hook, knocking Victor in the face. His whole body is thrown backward. Before his men can do anything, River has his guns out.

I notice we're causing a scene, and I don't like scenes. I motion for River to put his guns away.

"That was a fucking warning. We're done here."

Chapter Eighteen

Julianna

Whispers.

I've never noticed the whispers before, but as I walk around the clubhouse, they are everywhere. I don't know what has happened, but obviously no one wants to tell me.

"Why is everyone looking at me?" I ask my mom, who I find in the kitchen, washing up. She has always been the most dutiful wife and present mother, but I don't know who she is anymore aside from that. I don't think she knows either. We are like chalk and cheese, and although I love her to bits, our mindsets are completely different and sometimes it's hard for us to get on the same level.

She dries her hands, her pink nails sparkling before she turns to me. "I don't know what you mean."

Lips pursed, I lean back against the counter and study her. "I just walked in and everyone is staring and whispering about me. I came here because I was told it's a club dinner, not so that I could feel like a zoo animal."

She sighs and looks anywhere but in my eyes. Jesus Christ, what have I missed? "There was an incident earlier, and..." She trails off, looking to the doorway like she wants to run through it. She shakes her head. "It was nothing. Can you help me carry out the food?"

My jaw drops as she walks out with a fruit platter. My mom hates conflict, always has, which means that something is going on and she doesn't want to be the one to tell me. I grab a tray of the roasted vegetables and chase after her, stepping through the sliding door and placing the tray down on the table outside. She turns and heads back inside, and I stand there glancing around at the various people chatting and laughing outside, until my sister Veronica comes out of her room. When she sees me her eyes widen, and I quickly grab her arm and pull her next to me before she can run away, too.

"Can you please tell me what is going on?" I ask, brow furrowing. "Mom won't tell me and I'm seriously about to leave if no one talks to me." I look into her brown eyes and she looks...a mixture of guilty, sad and angry. "What is it?"

She leads me back inside the clubhouse, all eyes on us, and into her bedroom here. She closes the door behind us. "There's something I need to tell you."

"What?" I ask, my stomach sinking. "Just tell me!"

"I've been sleeping with Victor," she blurts out, covering her face with her hands. "We were seen kissing in public, and now everyone knows. And you know what this family is like—someone told Mom, and then Aunty Jo overheard, and then everyone was telling everyone."

Eyes wide, I slowly sit back down on the bed. "Well, now I know why everyone was staring and talking about me."

I know I should be hurt and betrayed at my sister's disloyalty, and part of me is, but more than anything I suddenly feel opportunistic. They can't expect me to marry him after this.

"How long has this been going on?"

She can't even look me in the eyes. "About two years. It happened right after my eighteenth birthday."

This makes my blood boil. That fucking predator. He preyed on my sister. Probably had some sick countdown. I will destroy him and I hope my father goes nuclear on him.

"I know you're supposed to marry him, but I think it's unfair. I should be the one marrying him, and I should lead the MC with him. Just because you happened to be born first doesn't make you any more worthy."

Well.

Fuck you, Veronica.

"What in God's name makes you qualified to lead the MC? Do you know how to balance the books? Do you know what the hell we do to make money? You sit at home making social media posts. You wouldn't know how to close a real estate deal if your life depended on it."

"Mom doesn't know that shit. She just plans events and attends to Dad. You can still do whatever you do."

"And be *under* you. Fuck. That. Shit. This club is mine. Not Victor's. Not yours. Mine."

We just stare at each other, and I realize I need to use this to my advantage. "Look, you should tell Dad that and see what he says," I suggest, wrapping my arms around myself. Who needs enemies when you have a sister like this? "You know Victor and I can barely stand each other and I don't want to marry him at all." In fact, I'm judging *her* for having such shitty taste in men, because Victor is an asshole. "But you really didn't care about me at all, did you? What if I did want to marry him? Thanks for letting me know that I can never trust you to have my back in any situation. And remember, one day *I* will be running this MC. Not you. Victor will step down before I do. Better yet, why don't you and Victor run away to be together and leave the Angels MC behind?"

"Victor would never do that," she replies, frowning. "And I didn't mean to hurt you, Julianna. But I love him. And he wants me to be his wife and stand beside him through all of this."

I grab her shoulders and turn her to face me. "Well, he doesn't get to have that. It's not his blood right, it's mine. You can take it up with Dad, by all means. Because I don't want to marry him. He's not the type of man I'd ever marry."

I storm out of the room and accost my mom in the kitchen. "So you expect me to marry Victor after the whole MC knows that he's been sleeping with Veronica?"

"Keep your voice down," she says, glancing behind me. "Your father doesn't know what happened yet, but when he does, he will handle it."

"So that's it?" I say, hands in the air. "Is Nanny here?"

"No, she wanted to rest."

Well, if she's not here, I'm leaving, too.

When I get in the car I can see that Romeo has texted me.

Johnny: What are you doing now?

Julianna: Just leaving the clubhouse. Lots of drama.

Johnny: Meet me at mine?

Julianna: On the way.

I'm glad he's not coming to me, just in case someone tries to come looking for me. I reverse out of the clubhouse's driveway and head to his instead. He opens his garage and I park inside, hopping out and running into his arms.

"What happened?" he asks, stroking my hair gently.

He leads me inside as I start talking. "Long story short, we had a family dinner. The vibe was off, everyone kept looking at me, and I knew something was up. Then I find out that Veronica has been sleeping with Victor, and now everyone knows. Oh, and she thinks she should be married to him. Now by all means she can have him, but she's not taking my place in the MC."

"Shit," he whispers, and I freeze, looking into his eyes.

"I can't take any more lies today," I say, enunciating every word. "Did you know about this?"

Because his "shit" was accompanied by a little flinch. One almost unnoticeable.

Almost.

"I heard a rumor," he admits, hand commencing with the stroking. "I didn't know if it was true, but yes, I did hear about it recently. And then today…"

"What happened today?" I ask, going cold. Why am I the last to fucking know everything?

"I saw them together when I went to go talk to Victor. They were, um…kissing."

"And why didn't you tell me?" I ask. "It's kind of us against the world right now, Johnny. And if we aren't rock solid, then this isn't going to work. We need to be honest with each other about everything."

He lets go of me and rubs the back of his neck. "I'm sorry, I should have told you."

"What else are you keeping from me?" I ask, moving closer and forcing him to look at me. "Just tell me. All I want is honesty no matter how much it hurts."

He takes a deep breath.

"I didn't tell you because I didn't want to bring it up," he says, grabbing onto my arm and holding me next to him as if he's scared I'm about to run away. "Because then I'd have to tell you that before you and I started seeing each other, before I even knew you as someone other than the person taking over the Angels... Rosalind and I were sleeping together."

I freeze.

Veronica sleeping with Victor didn't hurt. I don't care about Victor.

But this one?

This one fucking hurts.

Johnny was sleeping with my younger sister before me. I'm having her seconds right now, and I had no clue. Because no one fucking bothered to tell me.

Without another word, I turn around and head back to my car.

Fuck this.

Fuck everyone.

Chapter Nineteen

Romeo

I don't let her get very far.

I knew she'd be upset, and I also knew I should have told her sooner, but I didn't want to fuck things up. Waiting until now probably fucked them up even more.

"It never meant anything," I tell her, pulling her to a stop and backing her up against the hallway wall so she has no choice but to listen to me. "She came up to me at a party one night, we hooked up. It lasted a few months, and that was that. I never would have touched her if I knew that this would happen. I'm sorry I didn't tell you. I didn't even know she was your sister until that day I was in the closet. I figured you were distantly related, but that's it. I should have told you. And you're right, it *is* us against everyone, and we need to be able to trust each other a hundred percent. I fucked up by not being up front about this. But that is all I know. I swear."

Her beautiful blue eyes are hurt, and I hate that I've caused them to look like that. "I'm sorry," I whisper this time. "If I could go back, I would ignore her that night, trust me."

She must be feeling betrayed.

And I might not have a brother, but if I had only just found out she had slept with someone I was close to, like River or Matthew, I would be pissed. I wouldn't want anyone I know to have her in that way, which is why I should have told her at the start before all the feelings formed. Before I proposed.

"Do you understand what it feels like to know that you slept with my sister?" she asks, eyes narrowing. "Like shit! That's how it feels. It makes me actually feel sick."

"I didn't know you then," I tell her softly, letting go of her arms. "And now that I do, I don't want to touch another woman again! I'm not sure what you've done to me, but I only want you. And if you realize what I was like before, you'd realize how massive that is. It's like you've ruined me for other women! So I'm sorry I didn't tell you, but going forward you have nothing to worry about because I'm crazy about you."

I can tell she has shut down a little, but she's stopped trying to escape at least and is listening to my words. I hope she can forgive me because I truly mean everything I've said—it's not bullshit at all. I couldn't care less about Rosalind, not that I'd say that to her. But she really was just another body for me, whereas Julianna is just on a completely different level. I know that makes me sound like an asshole, but it's the truth.

"I need a minute," she says, and heads into my bedroom.

I fucking hate seeing her with anything other than a smile or pleasure on her face and it hurts worse that I put it there. But like I said, I didn't know we'd end up here, together, and unfortunately I can't change the past.

When I go into my bedroom about thirty minutes later, she's sitting there, on her phone, silently ignoring me. I know she wanted some time, but I just want to fix things.

"There's one other thing I want to tell you, just because we are laying it all out on the table," I say, sitting next to her. "Rosalind has been messaging me nonstop since we ended our little arrangement, which was the day your granddad died. I never once replied, but yeah, there is that."

She purses her lips. "Why is everything so hard? Being with you is hard."

"Does that mean you don't want to do this anymore?" *Please say no.*

She's quiet for a while, but finally says, "Leaving you would be even harder."

I go to her, wrapping her in my arms and kissing the top of her head. We stay cuddled like that for a few minutes in silence.

"Now, what did you want to talk to me about?" I ask her gently.

"Nothing," she replies, sighing. "It can wait."

"I have an idea..."

"What?"

"I think we should get married. Like now. Tonight. Soon."

She looks at me like my head just exploded.

"I know it sounds crazy, but you are the one I want to be with forever. And marriage would show how serious we are."

And no one could take it away from us.

I'm fucking scared about losing her and it's making me lose all rational thought.

"Johnny—"

"No, never mind. It's been a pretty fucked-up day for you," I mutter. "You should rest. Do you want to chill here? I can get us some food and drinks. Or I can take you out somewhere?"

"Staying here is safer," she says, and I nod.

"Okay, you stay here, I'll head out and grab us everything we need," I say, kissing her on the forehead. "I love you, Julianna. You're it for me."

As quickly as I can, I head to the store and get us some alcohol, soda, snacks and pizzas. I also get a beautiful bouquet of sunflowers, hoping they might cheer her up a little. I'm new to the whole putting-effort-into-romance thing, but for her, I'm willing to do anything.

When I get home though, she's gone.

"Fuck."

I don't even want to go chase after her, in case someone comes to her house. I pick up my phone and try to call her, but she doesn't answer, so I send her a text.

Romeo: I'm so sorry, Julianna. I'm here to talk when you are ready.

I send her a picture of the flowers, just so she knows I'm fucking trying, and then put them in a vase for when she returns.

If she returns.

The thought that she might not forgive me doesn't sit right with me, but I'm just going to have to give her a little bit of space.

Knowing that she hasn't eaten, I Uber Eats some food to her house. I don't know what else I can do.

My phone buzzes and I quickly grab it, thinking it's Julianna, but it's not.

River: Where are you? Come to the clubhouse. Shit has gone down.

"Fuck."
I grab my keys and head out.

Chapter Twenty

Julianna

I do feel bad just leaving his house, but I just had to get away to think. The whole day was a lot, and I need some space.

I drive to the park where he first helped me with my car, and sit down on a bench thinking about everything that has happened. The Victor and Veronica thing isn't even an issue anymore—it's the Rosalind thing that hurts. I have a lot of pride, and I'm not someone who would ever be with a person my family or friends have already been with; that's just not appealing to me in any way. Rosalind has seen him naked, knows how he makes love and has seen his cock.

I don't fucking like that.

At all.

What woman would?

I understand everyone has a past, and I know Johnny has been with a lot of women, and I'm okay with that. I just never thought that one of the notches on his belt would be my own sister.

Although today has shown me just how much my

sisters obviously don't have a good relationship or tell each other things going on in our lives.

What a mess.

All I know is that I'm not marrying Victor, and no one is going to make me. I don't care what my duty to this family is. My family haven't had my back at all, even my own parents. Everyone has their own agenda, and it's about time I realize that.

How would I feel if my dad did let Veronica take my place and marry her off to Victor? I would be relieved, but I also know that my rightful place is to lead the MC. He cannot change the rules of the Angels unilaterally. My father is not a Callisto. He does not have the power he thinks he does.

I'm the one who is business minded and brings the money in—Veronica wouldn't know how to do any of that. She'd play the dutiful wife, as she is much like our mother, but that's the only thing she would bring to the table. I think it would hurt to be replaced, just like that, just because I didn't want to marry that oaf.

I'm not giving up my title without a fight, that's for damn sure.

And then there's Johnny's idea. Getting married. Now. I mean, we *are* engaged. Technically. Would getting married be better or worse? Right now it seems better, but I know I need to think on it more.

I drive home only to find some food sitting for me at the door, with a note from Romeo.

I'm sorry.

I pick up the Chinese food and get inside my house,

my stomach rumbling. I didn't eat at the clubhouse, and then I left before I could eat at his.

Okay, that is pretty sweet of him.

This is our first fight, and I don't think I handled it too well, but again, it wasn't a regular fight, was it?

It's not every day you find out your sister and the man you see a future with had sex.

Julianna: Thank you for the food.

Johnny: You're welcome. Will you come over tomorrow so we can talk?

Julianna: Okay.

Johnny: Good.

Curled up on the couch, I eat my dinner and ignore the phone calls from my dad. I can speak to him tomorrow, because I don't have it in me to argue with him tonight, too.

The next morning I wake up to a lot of missed calls. From everyone. My dad, my mom, my sisters, Victor and Johnny.

What the hell is going on?

I text Romeo back first, asking him what was wrong.

Romeo: Victor started shit with the Devils last night. Tensions are high.

Fuck.

Julianna: Are you okay?

Johnny: I'm fine. One of my men, not so much. You just be careful. He's an asshole, and unpredictable. He's telling everyone he's the acting president of the Angels.

What? Surely Dad isn't going to be okay with that.

Julianna: You stay safe too. I'll see you tonight. Heading to talk with my dad now.

Throwing the sheets off me, I quickly get ready and drive to the clubhouse. I hear my dad before I see him. He's yelling, and hopefully at Victor. I linger in the kitchen, waiting for them to come out of their meeting.

"Hey," Damon says as he steps into the kitchen. He's freshly showered, in jeans and a white T-shirt. His dark hair is still damp and mussed. He's a good-looking man, and no one could deny that, but he also has a good vibe about him.

"Good morning."

He opens the fridge and grabs a bottle of water. "Come to hear about the shit show?"

"Something like that."

"Hello," I say when Dad steps in and sees me. "Is everything okay?"

He comes over and gives me a hug. He has always given the best ones. "I'm glad you're here. Seems we have a lot to talk about."

"We do. What happened last night? I had missed calls from everyone."

We both take a seat at the table, and Damon takes his leave. "Some things went down and I wanted to make sure you were okay. I heard about everything that happened with Veronica."

"Did she come and speak with you?" I ask, gauging his reaction, but as usual he gives nothing away.

"She did. And I know this has turned into a very... uncomfortable situation." He winces, crossing his arms and leaning toward me. "I know you didn't want to marry him anyway, and now she does, so it puts me in a very tight situation."

"Is she going to take my place?" I ask. "I mean, I would love for her to do so in the marriage, but not my title as firstborn daughter. *My* husband is to be president. Whoever that is. I would be a good leader, and you know it. I've been getting ready for this for my whole life. I went to business school just for this."

"We will follow tradition" is all he says, but I don't know if he's referring to me still marrying Victor or me being allowed to marry someone else and have him as president.

I want to ask him about Victor claiming he is president already, but then he will ask where I heard that information.

And yeah, I do *not* want to go there. Not yet.

"So what now, then?" I ask, almost scared of the answer. "You can't expect me to marry Victor after all of this has come out. You didn't see the way everyone was looking at me. I have my pride, Dad. And I'm not going to be with someone my sister loves and wants to marry herself."

He runs his hand through his blond hair, and I can tell he has no answers for me. "Leave it with me, I will find a solution. I know you think Victor is so easily replaceable, but I've also been preparing him for this role for years, Julianna. Years. Who else is going to take over from me?"

Me, I want to scream.

Me.

I can do it, and I can do it better than that Neanderthal. I can do it by my damn self.

But I know Dad won't listen. He's stuck in the old ways, and my ideas are too outlandish for him.

But soon he will see that there is no other option.

It's my time to shine.

Chapter Twenty-One

Romeo

My day went from shit to worse.

When I got back to the clubhouse, River broke it down for me. They had all gone out to the local biker bar, and Victor had been there with a few of the Angels MC. When he saw River, Jeremiah, Matthew and Train there, he came right up to them and started a fight, hitting Matthew in the face, breaking his nose, and screaming at them that now that he's acting president, things are going to change around here. He said the Angels no longer owe the Devils any money and they wouldn't be paying any longer.

We all know he is fucking lying, because Julianna isn't married to him, and never will be if I have my way. The man sounds unhinged. While we have had a chaotic past with the Angels, things have changed and it has been mostly passive until this. Despite what happened, Mikey and my grandfather actually coexisted peacefully. Now that Mikey is gone and the debt is ending, all is going to shit.

Victor started a war, and for no damn reason, unless he has a plan no one else knows about. Maybe he knows his only chance of being president is hanging by a thread, that thread being Julianna and the fact she would rather lose it all than marry him.

I don't like knowing that shit is about to get hectic with the Angels MC and people Julianna may care about or consider family could be in danger. But more than anything I just need to make sure that she is okay and won't get caught in the crossfire.

As president I'm not only put in the position of having to deal with this in a way that appeases the men, but also doesn't escalate a fucking war. I wish Victor could stop trying to start shit just because he's in some kind of power struggle.

I have a few options here. I could:

1. Reach out to the actual president—Julianna's father, Paulie—and discuss.
2. Hunt Victor down and teach him a lesson.
3. Play it dirty and take down a group of them.
4. Marry Julianna and we join the clubs and rule them together.

They are going to love the idea of me fucking their future queen.

Not.

As much as I want Option Four, I know that is something that is currently not on the table. So I need to consider the other three. My instinct is to go with Option One because it is the most diplomatic. But I have the older men like Trent watching my every move right now, and I can't show any weakness.

I'd personally like to do Option Two, for more than one reason. I'd love nothing more than to teach Victor a lesson, especially for how he has disrespected Juli-anna with Veronica.

"What you thinking?" River asks from where he's leaning against the wall, one leg up. He looks like he's asking about the weather, not what we are going to do in revenge.

"I'm torn," I admit. "I want to teach him a lesson, but I also think we should speak to Paulie and let him know that his golden boy thinks he's calling all the shots already and starting shit he won't know how to finish. I'm thinking we do both. Speak to Paulie, then depending how that goes, get Victor."

River nods slowly. "I like it. Let's hope Paulie can manage this situation before it gets way out of control."

None of us mind a good fight. And I have no problem going at Victor with guns blazing. Figuratively and literally.

But starting a war means innocent people getting hurt, and us having to watch our backs constantly. It means us having to overprotect the women and children, and it really does bring out the darkness in each of us.

We don't want war.

But we also aren't afraid of one.

We also can't let Victor do whatever the fuck he wants without any repercussions. And threatening not to pay us our cut? Fuck that.

Maybe Paulie will let me take him one-on-one. Yeah, I'd like that.

Julianna can watch. And know that she is choosing to be with the right man. The thought makes me semi hard. I smile to myself at that, flashing my teeth in an evil grin.

"What the fuck are you smiling like that for?" River asks, amusement in his tone.

Fuck, I forgot he was still standing there.

"Just thinking about beating the shit out of Victor," I say, standing up from the table and walking past him. "Best-case scenario, Paulie agrees he deserves his ass kicked."

River steps next to me as we walk outside to our motorcycles. "He's supposed to be a decent fighter, but you are going to humble him real quick. I wouldn't want to fight you, that's for sure."

"Funny, I always think the same about you. Maybe that's why we get along so well."

We share a wide grin and do a little fist bump.

"Does your dad know about what happened?" Jeremiah asks as he joins us. He's sporting a cut lip and a slight black eye from the fight. "Because he's walking over here right now with your grandpa and grandma."

Shit.

"What are you doing about all of this?" Dad asks me, scowling.

"Hello to you, too," I say in a dry tone. "Grandma, Grandpa…"

"Hello, Johnny," Grandma Cathy replies, smiling.

"I'm going to speak to Paulie first, and go from there," I admit, waiting for him to tell me that I'm an idiot and I should just go in there guns blazing, but he actually agrees with me.

"Yeah, start there, at least then we can say that we tried to keep the peace. But after that we need to set an example and let them know that we're not going to let shit like this slide. We can't show any weakness. They get one chance to make this right, but if it's war they want, then we will give it to them."

"Paulie has made a bad decision with his successor," Grandpa Johnny adds, shaking his head. "Victor sounds like bad news."

"I think you are making the smart choice," Grandma says, wrapping her arm around her husband's. "Let them handle Victor—he's their man, not yours."

I couldn't agree more.

That night Julianna comes over and parks in the garage. It used to be exciting having her hidden away here, but now I'd love nothing more than to show her off. To take her out on dates and just enjoy everyday life with her.

But I'll take what I can get.

I open the car door for her and she jumps into my arms, holding on to me. I hope this means that she has forgiven me, or maybe she just needs some comfort. Either way I'm just happy that she's here, safe, and she must not exactly hate me if she's holding on to me as tightly as she is.

"I really am sorry," I tell her as she pulls back and looks up at me. "I love you, Julianna. And I'm not going to do anything else that can mess us up. You are it for me, and anyone before you doesn't even fucking count anymore."

Blue eyes widen at my declaration. "I love you, too."

Lowering my head, I kiss her gently, cupping her cheeks with my palms. I then kiss her forehead.

I don't know how we are going to play this game and win, but to me, I've already won.

"We have a lot to talk about," she says, moving out of reach of my hands as they start to roam. I turn and follow her as she enters my house and sits down on my leather couch. "First of all, I think we need to talk to my grandma. We need her on our side. And she told me some things before and..." She trails off. "She knows about you and me. My dad knows I'm not going to marry Victor, but right now Veronica is fighting to take my place, so I need to play it carefully."

Hearing her declare that she's refusing to marry that asshole makes me extremely content.

"We're going to have a meeting with your dad to discuss Victor, and just to see where we all stand. If he keeps going out and starting shit, it's going to be a war and it's going to get messy," I add, taking her hand and running my thumb along her knuckles. I bring her hand to my lips and kiss it. "Tell me what your grandmother said about us."

"She told me the truth about what happened with her, Johnny and Mikey," she says, and then tells me about how Johnny's father, my great-grandfather, essentially ruined their love story by threatening her, and how she then married Mikey in turn.

"That's fucked-up," I mutter, wondering what this information would do to Grandpa Johnny. "I don't want anything like that to happen to us."

"Me either," she says, moving closer to me and pressing her body against mine. "We can't let anyone come between us. And people are going to try to, from all sides." She straddles me and pushes down against my cock. "We need to be unbreakable."

I pull her down to me with my hand on the back of her neck and say against her lips, "We are."

And then I kiss her lips, and her forehead. She smiles at me.

"Have you given any thought to my idea? About getting married. Sooner rather than later?"

She kisses me again. "Let's talk to my grandmother first."

That wasn't a no.

Chapter Twenty-Two

Julianna

Hours later I'm at the clubhouse, biding time till we go talk to my grandmother and having flashbacks of Johnny fucking me over the couch, when Victor himself walks in. I'm sitting with my mother, so he's on his best behavior, and the pretense of it all makes me feel sick.

"How are you, Julianna? You look beautiful today," he says, sitting next to us.

"Thank you," I reply, knowing that the glow is not from or for him. "I hear you've been out causing a little chaos."

He shrugs. "They were talking shit, and I couldn't let that slide. A new era is starting, and we need to make sure that the Devils know who's boss around here."

"And what about you sleeping with my sister?" I ask, and my mom chokes on her coffee.

"Julianna," she chastises.

"What?" I ask, pursing my lips. "Everyone knows what is going on, we might as well talk about it."

"I think that is more of a private conversation we should have," he says, showing no remorse of any kind.

"And as of yet we are not officially married, and it was your decision to hold off."

"But yours to stick your cock into my younger sister."

"Julianna!" Mom now growls, grabbing a hold of my arm. "Can you please stop being so vulgar? You can both discuss this at another time."

When she's not present, so she doesn't have to deal with the truth of the situation.

"She's right," Victor agrees, his brown eyes unhappy with me, and his jaw tight with his unwavering disapproval. He reaches out to comfort my mom with a hand on her shoulder. "We don't need to upset your mother with our private issues. We can go into another room and talk about this now, if you'd like."

I'd rather eat my own fucking eyeball.

"Maybe another time," I tell him, forcing a smile that is all teeth. "I'm about to help cook dinner and to be honest I think I need a little time to process the whole thing. There seems to be a lot going on right now, don't you think?"

He nods. "Yes, there does. I'm available to have a conversation whenever you are ready. Or maybe you can let me know when you want to go on another date."

"Will my sister be joining us?" I ask, flashing him a saccharine-sweet smile.

My mom looks like she'd rather be anywhere else, and being the proper woman she is, I know she must be horrified, but guess what? This is happening. This is our reality, and there's no point trying to sweep it under the rug.

"If you want," he replies, keeping a straight face.

My mom excuses herself and leaves the kitchen, and

Victor leans closer to me. "We're getting married. Don't try to use Veronica to get out of it."

"How can you marry me and love her? That's messed up."

"I don't have to love you to marry you. We can be married in name only, if that's what you want. We can have sex until we conceive a son to be the next heir and then go on with our lives."

I'm absolutely flabbergasted that he thinks this is an okay plan. This man is so power hungry that he reeks from desperation, and he is the last man I would want to be the father of my child.

"Wow, what a wonderful offer," I reply, getting up to leave. He acts like he has all the power and like I need him, but I don't. In fact, I'm trying to get away from him but he won't let me.

Some fresh air is just what I need, so I head outside and sit down on the veranda, glass of wine in my hand.

"Long day?" I turn around to see Damon standing there, gray eyes on me. He's a good-looking man, probably the best the Angels MC has to offer, and he's only a little bit older than me.

"You have no idea," I reply, taking a sip of wine. "I need this drink."

He laughs and sits next to me. "I hear you're about to be married. That sucks, you know. I always thought you were the hottest sister."

My lip twitches. "I bet I am the most appealing sister. For all the men who want to be president, anyway."

Damon shrugs and stretches out his jean-clad legs on the table, his black leather biker boots resting on the wood. "For some. Not all of us want extra responsibilities."

"That's refreshing to hear," I say, placing my glass down and turning to him. "Tell me, were you there at the bar when Victor started throwing punches and proclaiming that he's already president?"

"I wasn't, no. But trust me, I've been hearing all about it," he replies in a dry tone. He runs his hand through his dark hair, opens his mouth, and then closes it.

"What is it?" I ask.

"The Veronica thing..."

"Ah, yes. That," I mutter, picking up my glass again and finishing the rest of it. "I have to admit that I didn't see it coming, but I wish nothing but the best for the happy couple."

Damon's brow furrows in confusion. "You don't care?"

"I don't want to marry Victor," I admit, lowering my tone. "So if those two want to be together, it solves pretty much all of my problems right now."

Well, that's not exactly true, but he doesn't need to know that. There's also the situation of "me being in love with the president of our rival MC," but that's a whole other thing, isn't it?

"That's pretty fucked-up," he says after a few moments of silence. "I thought maybe you liked Victor. I mean, some women are into that whole big, brooding, older man thing."

"Yeah, the daddy thing? Veronica sure is. Me, not so much. In fact, I couldn't think of anything worse."

He laughs out loud. "That she is. So what are you going to do?"

"I have no idea. Watch this space, though, because things are about to get very interesting," I comment, studying him. "And you better not repeat anything I have just said."

"Our conversation stays between us," he promises, putting his hand over his heart. "And I don't want you going anywhere—my bank account has been nice and fat since you started all these investment properties. It feels nice to be legit, for once in my life, and not have to worry about cops coming after me."

I blink slowly. "I don't even want to know."

He smiles, showing off straight white teeth. The Angels MC tattoo on his neck does give him that criminal vibe, but his eyes are warm and kind, and I've always liked that about him. "You're too good for this place, you know that?" he says as he stands, pulling a smoke out of his jean pockets. "Don't let anyone else let you think otherwise."

He flashes me a wink and walks back inside. I think that's the nicest thing anyone here has said to me, but it also offends me.

This club is meant to mean more to people, and if I was running it, it would.

Instead we've got an episode of *Jerry Springer* playing out, and I'm so over it.

Chapter Twenty-Three

Romeo

There's nothing better than a long motorcycle ride to clear your head. I love riding with my MC—the only thing that could make it better is if Julianna was on the back, pressing her soft breasts against me. But as we're about to go and meet with her father, it's probably best to get her out of my head.

We meet at a neutral biker bar, me with two of my men, and him with two of his. Of course he brings Victor, who I was hoping would be grounded at home for all the shit he has started.

"Paulie," I say, offering my hand. He takes it and we shake. See, amicable. I can do this.

"Romeo," he replies with a nod.

We step into a private room, the door loudly shutting behind us, and then we all take a seat. River and Matthew flank to my sides, and Victor and Damon sit on either side of Paulie. Damon is a good man. Not a loose cannon like Victor. I'm surprised Paulie didn't choose him for Julianna, although I'm glad he didn't. He's a good-looking motherfucker.

"I just thought we could sit and talk about what happened the other night, before it turns into something we can't contain," I start, sitting back and studying Victor. "As I hear it, your man started a fight with one of the Devils, Matthew here, and attacked him, stating that he is the president now, and things are about to change. So I just wanted to ask if you are aware of what your man is doing in the name of your club."

Paulie's lips tighten, and his eyes dart to Victor and back to me. "I've heard about the incident, but Victor states that he did not start the fight. And he said he didn't claim he was the president of our MC."

Victor's smug brown eyes look back at me, and I can see that he has Paulie completely wrapped around his finger. Maybe he sees Victor as the son he never had, I don't know, but fortunately I came into this prepared for this type of bullshit.

"So who started it, then?" I ask Victor. He nods toward Matthew, who everyone knows wouldn't hurt a fly unless he had to, and has never started a fight in his life. "So you're saying my cousin here came right up to you and started a fight for no good reason?"

Victor nods. "Yes, he did. Maybe he knew I'd be taking over soon and wanted to test me and our club. I don't fucking know. But I would never start shit for no reason—I'm aware of how important the treaty between our clubs is."

Paulie looks at Victor, approval in his eyes. "Exactly right. We don't need to go backward. We don't want anyone else getting hurt, so perhaps you can speak to your men about starting fights when they see members of the Angels MC out in public."

Wow, he really just believes anything Victor says. Poor man.

"And Damon, what did you see?" I turn, testing his integrity and loyalty.

He clears his throat, then says, "I wasn't there. I only know what I heard."

I nod. At least he didn't lie. He's diplomatic.

"I thought Victor might have his own version of the events, so I took the initiative of getting the actual surveillance footage from the bar," I say, flashing my teeth at Victor. "Just so you can keep going on and telling everyone how our club started it."

Victor doesn't break character. "We don't need to see anything—"

"I think we do," River says with an evil smile. He pulls out his phone and presses play, laying the phone out in front of Paulie.

In the video you can clearly see Victor be the aggressor, and you can hear him say the words, "I'm the president now, and things are about to change around here. We are not paying the Devils another dime."

The evidence finishes, and the room goes quiet. "I can send it to you if you want to examine it further," I say as the tension builds, making the air thick and uncomfortable.

Paulie slams his fist down on the table, because he knows he's fucked up. Not only did Victor start shit with us, he lied about it and now they all look like idiots.

I'm always one step ahead.

Especially when I know I'm dealing with sly bastards with no honor like Victor.

"Okay," Paulie says, looking me in the eye. "What do you want to make this go away? I don't want a war breaking out just as the new presidents step in. The

Angels will of course continue paying what the treaty states. Victor was mistaken."

Is he seriously thinking of still making Victor president after this?

After sharing a look with River, who knows I'm getting exactly what I want right now, I state my terms. "I think we need to make an example out of Victor."

"That is bullshit—" Victor yells.

"Your lies were bullshit."

He goes quiet.

"I was going to suggest a fight—"

"I'm in," Victor says, but I hold my hand up.

"But that's so barbaric. And we are not barbarians, are we, Paulie? I don't want Victor to be president. That's my stipulation. I'll forgive all this if he does not become prez."

Victor looks like he's about to explode. "You're fucking crazy if you think…"

"Romeo, you have no say in who the Angels' president will be," Paulie replies, standing up. "I apologize for Victor's behavior, I don't know what power trip he was on, but that won't be happening again. But your stipulation is out of line."

"Rumor has it your own daughter doesn't even want to marry this one. Seems like I'd be doing you a favor," I say, standing up as well.

"That is Angels business, Romeo, not yours."

"That's what I want, Paulie. Either accept that or the treaty is over."

He nods and then reaches out to shake my hand. "We'll get back to you tomorrow."

They leave the room first, and River turns to me, amusement on his face. "You got what you wanted."

"I usually do." I grin, and slap Matthew on the back. "Thanks for coming."

"No problem," he replies. "I have to admit, I wish I could've watched you annihilate him."

It's been a while since I've been in a proper fight, and to be honest I was kind of looking forward to it.

I hope I did us more of a favor than create a bigger problem.

Chapter Twenty-Four

Julianna

"Johnny's coming here now," I tell Nanny, who is baking away in her kitchen. "I just hope Mom or Dad don't suddenly show up."

"I doubt it; I think they've had enough of me," she replies with a grin as she wipes her hands on a dish towel. "Well, at least there will be plenty of food to offer him. If anyone does show up, we can hide him somewhere, I'm sure."

"I'm excited for you to meet him."

Especially since I haven't been able to introduce him to anyone. It's nice, and feels, dare I say it...normal.

"I'm excited, too. I remember seeing him at the funeral. He looks just like his grandfather," she says with a wistful look.

"Yeah, kind of weird how that all worked out," I comment in a dry tone, looking down at the bowl of batter in front of me and dipping my finger in for a taste. "Maybe we were meant to learn from what happened with both of you."

"Sounds like fate to me," she says, just as we hear his motorcycle rumbling toward the house. I open the garage for him and he rides right in, wearing his black jeans, leather boots and jacket but not his cut. He gets off and removes his helmet, then runs a hand through his thick, dark hair.

He's so damn sexy.

And then I'm in his arms and glancing up at him with a grin. "I'm sorry it's been an asshole of a day for you, but I'm glad you're here."

"You're already making my day better," he says, pressing his lips against mine. He then turns and pulls out a bouquet of flowers from his saddle. "And I couldn't show up empty-handed to meet your Nanny."

Smiling, I take his hand and lead him inside and into the kitchen. "Something smells delicious," he mutters.

"We've been baking."

I stop and Nanny turns around to face us. "Johnny, this is my grandma, Libby Rose, and Nanny, this is my love, Johnny."

"Nice to meet you, ma'am," he says, presenting her with the flowers.

She smiles as she takes them. "And nice to meet you too, Johnny. And please, call me Libby."

"Libby," he corrects.

She stares a bit longer at him, lost in a memory. "I'm sorry, where are my manners? Have a seat," she commands, and he does as he's told. "I'll make some coffee. Julianna, put some of the cookies and cake out for him."

I also do as I'm told and put some slices of cake onto a serving tray to place on the table. Johnny and I sit there and smile at each other until Nanny returns with the coffee. "Sugar?"

"Two, please," he replies, and she scoops out two spoons, stirs it and hands the mug to him. "Thank you."

"You are welcome. I know you've probably heard this a million times now, but you really do look just like Johnny Boy," she says reverently, studying Johnny's features.

"Julianna told me the truth about what happened with you both," he admits in a gentle tone. "I'm so sorry it didn't work out for you guys." He pauses, and then adds, "Well, maybe not. Otherwise Julianna and I may not exist or we'd be related." At that thought, a sour look crosses his face.

Nanny laughs out loud. "You know, that's a good point. So maybe it all played out how it was meant to. Do you both have a plan about what you are going to do?"

"I do, but Julianna hasn't told me how she feels about it. But... I think we should get married. It can be in secret, but I think we should do it. I love her with all my heart and there is no other woman out there that I want to be with for the rest of my life."

Grandma smiles, her eyes lighting up. "And that's all I've ever wanted for Julianna. I mean, for all of my granddaughters, but especially for Julianna. But I do have to ask: if you get married now, how do you plan on handling the two clubs? While I know how Paulie and the Angels feel about the Devils, how would your father, and grandfather, feel about you marrying the heir to the Angels?"

He takes a sip of his coffee and a bite of a cookie, but I know he's just biding his time to come up with an answer. "I think they'll be surprised and I think there will be a lot of logistical questions. If the two heirs of the two MCs get married, what does that mean? Correct me if I'm wrong, but according to the Angels charter, the oldest child of the president, even if she is female, inherits the presidency."

My grandmother nods.

"And if she is female, the man she marries automatically becomes president. So technically, if Julianna and I get married, I become president of the Angels too?"

"I want to add that nothing in the charter says a woman cannot lead the MC. It's a bit murky." Nanny takes a sip of her tea. "I left it vague on purpose."

"What?" Johnny and I both say at the same time.

Is she saying that she wrote the charter?

"Sweet pea, the only reason people think that's the rule is because your mother had no business running the MC. My Jenny Belle is sweet and kind and bighearted. Much like Veronica. So your grandfather and I implied that whoever married her would become president."

"Nanny, how did you not tell me this before?" As much as I love my grandmother, I cannot believe she kept this from me. She knew I didn't want to marry Victor and preferred to run the club on my own.

My grandmother wrings her hands. "I'm sorry, sweet pea. I just didn't want you to be burdened with running the club. You love what you do with the real estate. I didn't want you to have to lead a bunch of men on top of that."

As hard as I try, I cannot stay mad at my grandmother. I love her too much.

"Well, this changes things," Romeo says, and looks at me.

"I think we need to figure out what the best step forward is. Later." I raise my eyebrows at him and he understands.

Johnny and Nanny chat and just get to know each

other. It feels so easy, and it's just nice to have someone on our side. I can tell that she likes him, but even more I can tell that she likes seeing me happy.

I mean, what more can you want for someone you love?

An easy love was never in the cards for me, but a true love always was.

Romeo's phone starts going off and he has to rush back to the clubhouse. Before he leaves, he tells Nanny how much he loved meeting her, and he's so glad that I have her to look out for me. When he's gone, I sit back down and wait for her to give me her thoughts.

She takes a sip of her coffee. "I think he's perfect for you, Julianna. He's smart and so sweet to you. And he is not power hungry. And he's extremely handsome. We obviously have the same taste in men."

I cover my mouth as I laugh. "I'm glad you like him. He's pretty wonderful. I honestly don't know how we got here, but I'm crazy about him."

"I can see that. And if you do get married, I'd like to be your witness."

When he first mentioned getting married in secret, I laughed it off. But the more he keeps bringing it up, and with Nanny's approval, the more sense it makes. If I'm already married, I cannot be forced to marry anyone else. And Victor cannot be president.

Sometimes the crazy options are the only ones.

"You did what now?" I whisper-yell when Romeo gives me a breakdown on what happened at their meeting with my father. We didn't have time at Nanny's for him to fill me in. We're both lying in his bed, naked, facing each other. "So you told him you didn't want Victor president and the beef would be over? Do you think he'll go for it?"

I don't know what my father will decide. On one hand, he does not like to be told what to do by anyone. On the other hand, he does not want to go to war. He knows we have too much to lose.

Johnny just laughs and pulls me closer, like we're talking about something cute instead of the fact that he's thrown my father's master plan up in the air.

"Babe, but what if my father agrees to your stipulation?"

"What do you mean? That would be the best outcome."

"No, it wouldn't." I sit up. "He'll just pick someone else for me to marry. And no, it will not be you."

Johnny goes white, realizing what he did. "Shit, I didn't think of that."

"We need to get married."

"I know."

"Right now."

"Now?" Johnny looks like he has whiplash from all the twists and turns.

"You were right. We need to get married. It will solve all our problems. And Nanny said she'd be our witness. We can do this."

"Julianna, I don't want to take your power. I want to marry you for you—"

I put my hand over his mouth. "Yeah yeah yeah. Johnny, I know you love me and you didn't ask me to marry you because of this. And I want to marry you, too. But if we get both clubs on top of being married, it is a win-win."

Johnny kisses me. "Are we really doing this?"

I nod. "I want to."

"Then what are we waiting for? We do live just outside of Las Vegas, the home of quickie weddings."

"Should I call my grandmother? Should we do it now?" I lean for my phone to call Nanny. "It's only eight p.m.; she should be up."

I can't believe it, but I'm marrying Johnny Montanna. Tonight.

It might not be the wedding I envisioned as a child, but the man I'm marrying is more than I could have ever hoped for. And my tight, sleeveless, A-line gown is my dream dress. With a white-and-pink bouquet in my hands, I walk toward Johnny, Elvis standing behind him, waiting to marry us.

I never thought I'd be thinking those words, but I don't care who marries us, or who is here to watch, I just want to be Johnny's wife. Nanny is sitting in the front row of the chapel, wearing a baby blue dress. Johnny's so handsome in his black suit, and although I feel a little nervous, I know that this is what I want. The gaze in his eyes tells me that he feels the same.

"You look beautiful," he says quietly.

I smile up at him and get lost in his eyes while the ceremony starts.

We both say I do, and leave the chapel as husband and wife.

I feel a dash of guilt, but that all fades away when Johnny pulls me into his arms.

I love this man, and no one is going to take that away from me.

Chapter Twenty-Five

Julianna

"I love you," I whisper, kissing my husband slowly. I press my body against his, my nipples brushing his chest.

"And I love you, my wife," he replies, rolling me over so I'm underneath him. We make love again, slower this time, and then we both get in the shower for another round of lovemaking. I'm on cloud nine. I never expected to feel this way about someone. And I never thought I'd feel so completely loved and understood in return. I'm not going to lie, he makes it difficult to want to leave him, and as an independent woman, it's a little hard to admit that to myself.

Afterward, I get dressed and go to the clubhouse, wanting to be around for when my father makes his decision. I run into Damon coming out of the gym, wearing nothing but a pair of basketball shorts low on his hips.

"You're here early," he comments, arching his brow. Sweat drips down his chest, but I keep my eyes on his face.

"Yeah, I have some business calls to make, so I

thought I'd head into the office," I lie. I'm here for the gossip.

"So you're not here because you heard what the Devils asked of your father and you're nosy and don't want to miss out on the action?"

My jaw drops in mock hurt. "Come on, is that what you really think of me? You think I'm going to waste my day lingering around here just for the gossip? You don't think I have a job to do, money to make for the club?"

Damon blinks a few times and then loses it laughing, bracing himself against the wall. "All right, Julianna. I'll be the first one to tell you when a decision is made. You can stop it with the Oscar moment."

I narrow my eyes and cross my arms, leaning closer to him. "Seriously?"

"Yeah, sure. I'll text you when we get the message." With that, he walks down the hallway to his room. Who knew it was going to be that easy? All I needed was an in.

"Good morning, my daughter," Dad says, beaming as he sees me, and kisses me on the forehead. He's wearing all black, his hair slicked back after a shower. "You look lovely this morning."

"Thanks," I say, glancing down at my high-waisted jeans, boots and red crop top. "Where's Mom?"

"She's in the shower. Your grandmother was asking for you—you should go and see her today."

Shit.

Of course she wants to see me. I'm guessing that she wants me to tell my parents about the marriage immediately. Maybe she's feeling guilty for being there and keeping it from everyone. I suppose things can't stay hidden forever. "Yeah, I will."

"Good."

I wander into the kitchen and pour myself some juice, my phone beeping with a text from Bella. We've both been playing phone tag with each other, and I've been meaning to call her back.

Bella: When can I see you? I need an update.

Smiling, I type back.

Julianna: I need an update too. What are you doing tomorrow? Have a lot going on today.

Bella: I heard! We haven't even talked about Victor and Veronica. Are you okay? Stay safe.

Julianna: I'm okay. Just waiting to find out what Dad is going to do with Victor. Damon said he'd tell me.

Bella: Hot Damon?

Julianna: To me he is simply Damon. Tomorrow?

Bella: Yes. Dinner?

Julianna: It's a date.

Veronica shows up to the clubhouse shortly after, crying her eyes out, her cheeks red and blotchy. I'm about to ask her what's wrong since she is getting what she wants. But Veronica has always been dramatic.

"Do you not know what happened?" she asks, sitting down next to me on the couch. "Why aren't you upset?

That monster Montanna told Dad he didn't want Victor to be president!"

I roll my eyes. The only thing monster about Johnny Montanna is his cock.

"I don't want to marry Victor. Why are you upset? If he's not president he can marry who he wants. You can have him." I'm not understanding the tears.

"But he said if he's not going to be president he wouldn't marry me!"

Ouch. That's cold. Karma. It's a real thing.

This was a civilized outcome for them. Romeo could have hit back at the Angels, and then another war would have started. This way it's only Victor that loses and no one else. Okay, maybe Veronica.

Veronica cries harder and our mom comes out to comfort her, hugging her tightly and telling her it will all be okay. Damon walks out and stops in his tracks when he sees Veronica having a breakdown, and shares a wide-eyed look with me. It's actually nice to have someone on my team in here. I escape into the office and end up doing some work after all, until Damon comes into the room.

"Your father made the call. It's a no-go for Victor."

Yes! I cannot believe he caved.

"Victor is going to go after Romeo to challenge him to a fight. He thinks if he kicks his ass, your father will reconsider," Damon says.

"What? Right now?" I need to tell Johnny that Victor is coming for him.

"Yes. Let's go," Damon says, and I jump out of my seat and rush after him.

"Why are you inviting me?" I ask, grateful but curious.

"In my eyes you're going to lead the Angels one day—you have a right to know when a member is going rogue. And Victor is going rogue."

"Does Dad know that I'm coming?"

"He will when he finds out what's happening and sees you there," he replies, amusement in his tone.

With all the Angels men gathering in the parking lot, getting ready to depart, I am indeed the only woman. I try to hide behind Damon, until we stop at his motorcycle.

"What's this?" I ask, frowning. "You said we are going in your car."

"Car has a flat tire, and everyone else is riding. We have to ride," he says casually, arching his brow when his gaze lands on my expression. "Unless you want to ride with Victor, of course."

"No thank you," I reply, turning back to Victor, who is chatting with a still-crying Veronica at the front door. Wow, they are just all out in the open now apparently. But I also don't want to show up to Johnny's fight on the back of another man's bike. Especially not a young hot one like Damon.

Fuck.

It would be worse, however, to show up on the back of Victor's bike, so I guess Damon is the better option.

Victor walks by and Damon calls out to him. "You mind if Julianna rides with me?"

His lips tighten, but then he shrugs as my sister also joins us, threading her arm into his. "Why would you mind, Victor?"

I kind of want to laugh, because Victor's expression says he does mind. Not because he likes me or anything, but because he still sees me as his property. But if he says that, Veronica will give him shit for caring what I do, and he obviously doesn't want to deal with that.

"That's fine, just get her there safely," he tells Damon, and then walks Veronica back to the house, trying to get rid of her. I hear her asking why I get to go and she doesn't, and he reminds her that she doesn't want to go, because she wouldn't be able to handle it and he doesn't need her distracting him.

I'm glad I don't have to ride with him, but I can't see Johnny liking me riding with Damon, because bikers are possessive about that. I know for a fact he wouldn't want me riding with anyone other than him, but I'm kind of shit out of luck right now. I send him a text, hoping he'll see it.

Julianna: Dad told Victor he wouldn't be president. Victor is coming to find you to challenge you to a fight. I'm coming, but I have to ride with Damon. On his bike. Don't be mad. Love you.

"I don't bite, I promise." Damon grins, handing me a helmet.

"Shit," I whisper as I put the helmet on. I don't want to distract Johnny either, making him angry before the fight. Maybe we won't even see him until we walk inside the warehouse, so it won't even be an issue.

Maybe.

I hop on and keep a respectable distance from Damon's hard body, and then we are off.

Time to watch my husband fight my betrothed.

Chapter Twenty-Six

Romeo

The Devils MC are all crowded around the warehouse, rocking their leather cuts proudly, waiting for the Angels MC to arrive. I haven't spoken to Julianna, so I have no idea if she's up to date on what's going on. I wanted to text her to let her know that Victor sent word he wanted a fight five minutes after I heard from Paulie, but I accidentally left my phone behind.

What I didn't mentally prepare for was to see her ride in on another man's bike. I know it's her the second the Harley rides in, her blonde hair blowing behind her in the wind. I'd recognize her anywhere. She gets off the bike quickly, probably because she knows how fucking pissed I'm going to be, and removes her helmet, glancing around as if looking for me. I then look back to the rider to see it's Damon, the notably good-looking guy who came into the meeting with Paulie and Victor yesterday.

Motherfucker.

They walk down the path and into the warehouse together, and I'm this close to switching opponents and fighting this guy. He's more my age, too. So why not? Hell, I'll fight them both.

I force myself to turn away, knowing I need to get myself together. But the image of her riding on the back of another man's bike is engraved into my brain, so I decide to use it to help me win this fight instead.

I will deal with Julianna afterward.

Victor arrives and eyes the makeshift ring the Devils MC made out of wooden planks and wire, and then turns to me as he runs a hand over his bald head. He looks confident, cocky even, and it's going to make this win that much better.

Julianna stands next to her father, who holds her close to him, and even though I try not to look at her, I fail. Our eyes catch and hold for a long few seconds, and I'm sure she can tell how fucking unimpressed I am with her entrance, but I'm also glad she's here.

And fuck, she looks good.

"You ready for this?" River asks from next to me.

"I was born ready," I reply, and he smirks.

"Let's do this, then."

I move to the ring and Victor follows suit. Before the fight starts, Victor says a few words. "Thanks for coming, everyone. I know Paulie was forced to make a decision. And I respect that decision. But I feel like I need to prove how worthy I am to be president of the Angels."

What a prick. It's my turn to say something. "I just want to say that I too respect Paulie's decision and would've expected the Angels would, too. But whoever wins or loses this fight, the violence ends here. We don't want anyone seeking revenge on anyone. This is going to make things even. All right? And if anyone disagrees, they can fight River next."

The Devils laugh at that, the Angels look unimpressed, but no one says anything.

I face Victor in the ring, and River stands between us. I don't know where he got it from, but he's brought a large digital timer with him, and he steps back and presses it, letting us know it's time.

We don't discuss any rules.

There are none.

Victor tries to grab me first, but I move back and punch him in the face when he leans forward. The crowd is going off at this point, both of our names being called by our clubs. Victor comes for me again this time with a punch. I move but not quickly enough, and it lands me in the shoulder. I kick my leg out and get him in the stomach, and he hunches over, recovering. I decide to let him. He glances up at me, hate in his eyes, but little does he know I'm just getting started.

With a yell, he suddenly rushes me and tries to get me in a headlock, and the two of us just keep going at each other. I get two more punches in on his cheek and he gets me in the stomach, which almost winds me completely. He throws a hard punch, I'm not going to lie. I manage to wrestle him down onto his back, straddle him and punch him in the jaw with all the strength I have.

Repeatedly.

When I get off him, he doesn't get up.

The first thing I do is look over at Julianna, whose eyes are already on me. She looks relieved, maybe that it's over, even though she's still clasping her handbag like it's a lifeline. River runs up and slaps me on the back, the Devils all cheering, while the Angels help Victor get up and out of the ring. As everyone starts to leave, I realize something.

I'd rather do a million fights than watch Julianna climb back onto that bike with Damon.

That hurts way fucking more.

"You barely look injured and he's bleeding out," River comments with amusement in his tone. He then follows my line of gaze to Julianna. "Stop it, brother. You are being way too obvious."

He pulls me out of the ring and distracts me from Julianna. I don't comment on his statement. He doesn't know that she's my wife.

It's a little hard, though, to deal with the fact she's not coming home with me right now. She's leaving with Damon, on his fucking bike like he's her man. The adrenaline pumping through me from the fight isn't helping right now either. I feel like I need to punch someone else, or go for a run or something.

Or have some dirty sex, but that clearly isn't going to happen for me right now.

Fuck or fight.

That is the mood I'm in right now.

River all but drags me away, and once everyone leaves, we do the same. He doesn't say anything, and I appreciate that.

When we get back to the clubhouse I see two texts from her.

Julianna: Dad told Victor he wouldn't be president. Victor is coming to find you to challenge you to a fight. I'm coming, but I have to ride with Damon. On his bike. Don't be mad. Love you.

Julianna: I'm sorry, it was ride with him or not come. And I didn't want to miss seeing you.

I type out a few replies but then delete them, still too angry to say anything to her. Instead, I hit the gym for an hour or two, then have a cold shower. She did text me before she was coming. I know I shouldn't be mad at her.

I don't think I've ever felt jealousy like this before, probably because I've never cared so much before.

It's not a good feeling.

Why do people actually search for this?

I feel like I'm going fucking insane.

Julianna: I know you're angry. I'm coming over tonight.

As I grit my teeth, my ego wants to tell her not to bother, but my dick has other thoughts. I do want to see her tonight. And she's my wife. I cannot run from her.

When I see her tonight, I'm going to show her just who she belongs to.

Chapter Twenty-Seven

Julianna

He's pissed, I know. I grew up in this world, so I know how bikers are when it comes to their woman riding with another man. But I didn't have any alternatives. And Damon and I are just friends. It's not like he's an ex, or someone who has any interest in me.

Anyway, I can imagine how tonight is going to go, but part of a good marriage is learning how to have arguments and problem-solving together. Have to keep the fights clean and the sex dirty, I once heard my dad say. I was kind of disturbed hearing that, but it does make sense.

Seeing Johnny today—he was amazing. He is so strong, and Victor didn't have a chance. It kind of turned me on seeing him like that, if I'm being honest, and I wanted nothing more than to leave with him and let him have his way with me. Or maybe we should have waited until everyone left and he could have taken me right there in the ring.

When we get back to the clubhouse and Veronica sees a bleeding and limping Victor, she cries and wallows and makes a scene, and proves to the entire clubhouse that she isn't emotionally strong enough to lead.

"Thanks for the ride," I say to Damon, who simply grins.

"Any time."

"I don't think so," I reply, and he laughs.

When I arrive at Romeo's that night, I have a plan, and let my maxi dress drop to the floor the second I step inside his house, revealing a tight leather bra, black lace panties and a smile.

"I know you're angry, but I didn't have any other option. Damon even asked Victor if I could and he said yes, so I didn't have any excuses that I could say out loud either," I rush out all in one breath. "It was ride with either Victor or Damon, and I'd rather Damon, who I'm actually friends with. So don't be angry. You know you are the only one I want. I am your wife."

His eyes narrow and the tension is still a little thick, but I don't miss the way his gaze roams over my body. He walks toward me and pushes me up against the door. "That's right, you're my wife. I don't want you on the back of another man's bike. Ever again."

"I know."

I wrap my arms around his neck and kiss him. He instantly grabs onto my hips and pulls me against him. I know it's a little toxic that I like that he's so possessive of me, and that he doesn't like seeing me with another man. But it's sexy.

He lifts me up and throws me over his shoulder like I weigh nothing, and carries me back to his bedroom, all but tossing me onto the bed. He rips off my lingerie like he can't wait one extra second without being inside of me, and I'm already wet and ready before he can even touch me. His big cock is pointing right at me, wanting in, and I stroke him once before he's on top of me.

The sex is hard, fast and passionate.

He lifts my legs up on his shoulders and goes in oh so deep, looking me in my eyes. Each hip thrust shakes the bed with the force, and the intense gaze in his eyes has me under his spell.

He's telling me that I'm his, and I'm taking it.

And loving it.

I trust him with my body, with my pleasure, and I never knew it could be like this.

I was born to be his, to be fucked by him, loved by him, protected by him.

He's mine.

After we've both come, he slides out of me and rolls me from my stomach onto my back, kissing me before lying next to me, both of us breathing heavily.

"I love you," I say, kissing his muscular bicep.

"I love you too," he replies, turning to face me. "And I'm glad you came today."

"More than once," I say, and he laughs.

"But seeing you on the back of his bike made me see red," he says quietly. "And I've never felt that way about a woman before, so it was pretty intense." He kisses my lips, and then says against them, "You are mine, Julianna. I love you like I've never loved anyone before. The only bike you'll ride on the back of is mine. The only cock you'll have inside you is mine. And you'll have my last name and my babies and I'll be the last man you'll ever be with."

I want all of that.

Pushing him back, I straddle him and look into his eyes, my blonde hair falling down over my face like a curtain. "I fucking love you, Johnny Montanna. I don't care what our family histories are. I'll do whatever it takes to be with you."

We make love again, slower this time, and fall asleep right after.

I wake up with my cheek pressed against his back, with me being the big spoon. As I open my eyes, I realize that we need to find a way to tell our families.

We can't stay in the shadows forever.

Romeo serves me breakfast in bed before I have to leave. "I have dinner with Bella tonight, but I'll see you after?"

"Sounds good," he says, kissing my forehead. "Stay safe, and call me if you need anything."

"I will. And...we need a plan to figure out what we're going to do."

He gives me one of his jaw-dropping smiles. "I know. Tonight we'll talk?"

"If you can keep your hands to yourself long enough for us to have the conversation."

He laughs. "I'll try."

The drive home is quiet, my mind racing with thoughts of how Romeo and I are going to make this work. Everything is up in the air, and for someone as organized and well planned as I am, I don't really like it. After I have a shower and get changed at home, I do some laundry and cleaning and then go to visit my grandma.

"Hey, where's Nanny?" I ask my mom, when she isn't in her room.

"She moved back into her old house yesterday," she explains, rolling her eyes. "I told her she should stay here, but you know her, never listens." She comes over to me and rests her hands on my shoulders. "And how are you doing, Julianna? I heard you left right after the fight yesterday. I'm not sure why you wanted to go. It must have been a lot to watch that. Poor Victor. He told me that he was sick—that's why he didn't do his best. I think he has the flu or something."

Yeah, I'm sure he does. How convenient.

"I wanted to see what happened," I explain. "Soon I'll be in charge of running the club, so I need to know how all of these things work."

She glances at me with...pity in her eyes. "You know the women don't deal with those things, whether you are married to the president or not. Your job will be to look after the men and inspire the women. You can organize the charity events and clubhouse parties. You don't need to be going to fights. There's a reason you were the only woman there—it's not the place for us."

We live in two different worlds, her and me.

"Things can change you know" is all I say in response, before I kiss her on her cheek. "I'm going to Nanny's."

When I pull up at her house, she's out the front watering the beautiful roses in her garden, and smiles widely when she sees me.

"Finally you came," she says, making a tsk-tsk sound. "I was worried about you."

"I'm fine," I promise her. "I want your help to figure out what we do."

We sit inside and have a chat over some tea. I give her the rundown on everything and ask her for her advice.

"I think you need to talk to Johnny's grandfather," she says in the end, a distant look in her blue eyes.

It's a scary thought to have more and more people

know about us, but if we want to be together, I know that it's something we're going to have to face.

Together.

When I get home I realize my house is more like my part-time accommodation right now. I'm barely here and just drop in and out to get ready. Everything has been so full on, and it will be nice when things start to slow down.

If they ever slow down.

Once I'm in my little black dress, heels and denim jacket, I grab my bag and go to meet Bella at the restaurant. She's there before me and sitting there looking at the menu.

"Hey," I say with a smile. She stands and we hug. "How are you? You look beautiful."

"Thank you, so do you," I reply, admiring her royal green crop and maxi skirt. "It's nice to finally see you after playing phone tag all week."

"I know." She smirks, leaning toward me. "And I don't even know where to start in catching you up on everything. Why don't you go first?"

I don't know where the hell to start either.

I take a deep breath. "I married Romeo, and I'm in love with him and no one knows except you and my grandma," I say, keeping a straight face.

She surprises me by laughing. "Very funny."

"I'm serious, Bella. This isn't a joke."

Wow, she mouths, and blinks slowly a few times. "Okay. That's a lot. You're married? To a Montanna?"

I nod and guzzle down the entire glass of wine the bartender just sat in front of me.

She laughs out loud. "What are you going to do, Ju-

lianna? Uncle Paulie will not love this. We're Callistos.
Are you going to merge the clubs?"

"I don't know yet, there's so many factors to take into
consideration. Victor, who is sleeping with Veronica,
and oh, then there's the fact that Romeo used to sleep
with Rosalind," I say, laughing at her shocked expression. "Us Callisto women really aren't making a good
name for ourselves, are we?"

She makes me explain all of that in detail, and then
we order our drinks and food while she processes that
information dump.

Three margaritas in, we are laughing and having the
time of our lives.

"What about you?" I ask her. "Dating anyone? You've
been mysteriously MIA these past few months, except
when I see you at work." Bella handles the money side
of the real estate business. I make offers and negotiate
contracts and Bella helps me finance the deals.

"Maybe," she admits, licking the salt from her lips.
"It's... River."

I arch my brow. "You're kidding me."

"Nope. Maybe this love grudge our families have is
really just fate saying we should be together."

"Oh my God, Bella. You don't know."

"I don't know what?"

"Nanny. She has always been madly in love with Romeo's grandfather. The only reason she married Poppy
was because Johnny Boy's father threatened her. Oh,
and Johnny Boy has no idea."

Bella puts her hand over her mouth in shock. "Holy
crap."

"I know. I think she should tell him. But she doesn't
want to disturb his marriage."

Bella orders another drink. "I have gossip. River tells me that his grandmother—I think her name is Cathy or something? She's a total bitch. I think Nanny should give her a run for her money. Speak of the devil." She picks up her phone, a smile on her face. "He said he's going to come give us a ride home later."

I look down at my now-empty cocktail glass. "I think he might need to."

I'm so happy for Bella and River, and I'm glad they don't have as much pressure on them as we do. Hours and multiple bars and drinks later, River finds us sitting at the bar, laughing so hard we're both almost crying.

He lifts Bella's face to him for a kiss, and then flashes a smile at me. "You sure you two are done? I can come back later if you want to stay longer." I'm jealous. Johnny and I can't do this. We can't be seen out in public. Sure, Bella and River need to be a bit cautious, but if they get caught they'll get a disapproving look. But me and Johnny? No way. It'd be the end of the world. This needs to end now.

"That's sweet, but it's pretty late," I reply, hoping that Johnny is still awake. If he's not he's about to be.

Julianna: You up? I'm going home.

Johnny: Yeah, I'm still at the clubhouse, but I can head to yours?

Julianna: That works. River is giving me a ride.

Johnny: I heard. I'm glad he's there to keep an eye on you both.

Julianna: Oh, by the way, Bella knows we're married.

Johnny: You know it's meant to be a secret right?

Julianna: Best friends don't count. Did you tell River?

Johnny: No, not yet.

Julianna: LOL. Men don't tell each other anything. We're leaving now. Come soon.

Johnny: Okay, baby.

"Aw," I say out loud, drunk me forgetting that River is right next to me. "He called me baby for the first time. Why is he so cute?"

I follow the couple out of the bar and walk to his car, sliding into the back seat.

He clears his throat before asking, "Where am I dropping you off?"

"My house, please," I say, telling him the address.

"No problem at all. And then back to yours?" he asks Bella, who nods.

"Yes," she replies as she reaches over to hold his hand while he drives.

The two of them are very cute.

When we get to my house I say bye to Bella and River walks me to my door, just as Johnny pulls up on his motorcycle.

"Fuck," he whispers, watching his president get off his bike. "So you are both really doing this."

"Yeah, I guess we are. I love him, River. You have no idea," I reply quietly.

"Shit is going to hit the fan."

"I know."

Johnny comes up next to me and pulls me next to him. "Thanks for getting her home," he says to River, who nods and heads back to Bella in his car.

"Thanks, River. By the way...we got married," I call out after him.

"What?" He spins around, gaping.

Johnny puts his hand over my mouth, takes my key and opens the front door for me. "We'll talk tomorrow." He waves River off and ushers me inside. "You had a good night, then?"

"I did, it was nice to catch up with Bella, and to just let loose a little."

I assume he's going to drag me into the bedroom and rip my clothes off, but instead he gets me some water and pain meds and helps me out of my clothes and tucks me in bed.

And then it's me who rips his clothes off.

Chapter Twenty-Eight

Romeo

A wonderful night with Julianna turns into an absolute fucking mess the second I return back to the clubhouse at seven a.m., sneaking back into my room like I was there for the entire night. They have to know that I come and go, but no one says anything. At least they haven't yet. I've sat down on my bed for about five minutes when my phone rings.

"Hello?"

"Hey, Romeo, it's Echo. We have a problem—could you come down to Devil's Play? Like now?" she asks.

She sounds a little scared, and Echo is never fucking scared.

"I'm on the way now. Are you okay?" I ask, sliding my shoes back on and heading back out the door.

"Yeah, just come now."

"Be there in fifteen."

On the way I call River and Matthew to meet me at Devil's Play. The second I pull up to the club, I'm shocked. Someone has set the place on fire, and while it's been contained by the firefighters, half of the building is now destroyed. Echo is standing out front, talking to a police officer. She turns and runs over when she sees me, and I open my arms and give her a big hug.

"Are you okay?"

She nods. "I'm fine, all the girls are fine. No one was here. We closed last night at four, and then I came back in the early morning to do some paperwork and it was on fire. I called the fire department, and they managed to put it out. Then the cops showed up. But look at it. Who would do this?"

I know exactly who would fucking do this. I just need the proof first.

"Come on, I'll get you home. Don't worry about the building, we can move the club somewhere else. All that matters is that no one was hurt."

River and Matthew show up just at that moment and rush over. I give them a quick rundown and then ask one of them to take Echo home while I speak with the police officers. It's not ideal that they showed up before me, but not much I can do about it. I tell Matthew to call the club and update them on what's going on. Victor may have hit other businesses of ours, but Devil's Play is definitely our most notable and successful.

I have no doubt it was him.

He lost the fight, the presidency, and now this is his revenge.

What a fucking coward, too.

I ask Echo to have her email me the security footage from the place because I want to see if I can find anything that can incriminate Victor, or any of the Angels he has on his side. She said that she couldn't since the police confiscated it and they'd return it in due time. I tell her to call our security company and ask for a copy.

This is exactly why I would have preferred to be here before the cops.

I send Julianna a quick text letting her know what's going on and ride back to the clubhouse. The first thing I need to do is find a new venue for Devil's Play to relocate to, and to get the new place up and running. I don't want anyone to lose out on money, the club or the dancers, and I sure as fuck don't want Victor to think that he's won this round. Everyone heads back to the clubhouse except me. I linger around and see if there's anything else I can find, but come up short.

When I do head back, River's standing out front when I get there and by the look on his face I can tell that something else has gone wrong. I'm going to need a strong drink.

"Tell me," I bark.

"Two bars have been hit."

"Fuck!" I grit out. "Cops took the security surveillance from Devil's Play before any of us could look at it, so we need to hit up the other places and see what we can find," I say, as my fists clench and release in fury.

"I'm on it," he says, and rushes back inside. I consider calling my dad, who is currently away with my mom on a damn vacation, but the last thing I want is for him to think that I can't handle the clubhouse without him.

It's my clubhouse now.

And I need to protect it.

The next day my baby cousin Corey decides to drop by to see me. She's only just turned eighteen and is very close to me; sometimes I used to babysit her for extra money when I was a kid.

"Hey, Ro," she calls out with a smile, using her nickname for my nickname.

I take a deep breath to calm myself before I respond. "Hey, Cor, how are you?"

"I'm good. You want to play some pool? I thought we could hang out. I haven't seen you in ages," she says, tucking her red hair back behind her ear. Her freckles are covered with makeup, but I always thought they were cute on her.

I consider telling her I just don't have the time for her, but fuck it. I could use a little break. "Always make time for family" is what Grandpa Johnny always says.

"Yeah, sure. Why not?"

We walk inside together and she starts chatting on and on, about college and her friends, and whatever else young people are into these days.

"I hear you're the president now. How does it feel?" she asks, setting up the pool table while I pour myself the drink I've been itching for.

"It feels pretty good," I admit, screwing the cap back on the bottle. "But it's also been extremely stressful. A lot of shit has been going down. Even today."

She pauses and frowns, as she chalks up her cue. "What happened?"

"Someone set a few of our businesses on fire," I explain. "Among other things. But it will be fine. I'll handle it. You be careful out there, all right? Things are getting a little tense with the Angels MC."

She nods. "I know. I never tell anyone about my connection to the Devils, so I can stay incognito. No one at college knows, aside from my best friend. You want to break?"

I shake my head. "You go ahead."

She breaks and sinks two balls.

Little pool shark.

We play three games and then she heads home. River gets back to me with the footage I need and we both watch it together. We see two men entering and spreading gasoline and lighting it. The whole thing caught on tape. The issue? They are covered from head to toe, including their faces with a balaclava. But going from the build of one of the men, it looks exactly like Victor.

"Now what?" I ask, narrowing my eyes on the screen. "I know in my gut it's him. Same height, same size. It's fucking him."

"I agree," River replies, cracking his knuckles.

"I'm going to put some eyes on him, have him followed," I decide.

And maybe Julianna can get me some inside information. If it is Victor, and I'm one hundred percent sure it is, he needs to be taken care of and now.

"He's one bold motherfucker," River mutters, slapping me on the back. "But don't worry, we'll get him. If it's war he wants, he doesn't know what he's starting."

Chapter Twenty-Nine

Julianna

I finish up some work, have dinner at my desk and then get ready to head to see Johnny. I see Victor and Veronica sitting and watching a movie together, along with a few other members. I don't think anyone will notice me missing, they will just assume that I've gone home. I return to my office to grab my phone charger and Damon finds me there.

"You heading home?" he asks, leaning against the doorframe. His gray sweatpants leave nothing to the imagination. Not that I'm looking in that direction, but come on, it's hard not to see. I'm a happily married woman.

"Yeah. What's up?" I ask, brow furrowing.

He pushes off the frame and comes into my office, pulling out a chair and sitting down. "Nothing. Just seeing how you are doing."

"I'm good. And yourself?"

I get the feeling that he wants to tell me something but doesn't know if he should. He doesn't know if he can trust me, and I don't know if I can trust him.

"Your dad heard the news about some fires that have

been happening to the Devils MC businesses," he finally says, shrugging.

So that's what he wants to talk about. "Who did the fires?"

Damon shrugs again, his gray eyes giving nothing away. "I don't know, but it's a little suspicious, don't you think?" I don't know if he's coming to me for information, or to give me information.

"It doesn't matter what I think. I'm just here to look pretty and make all of the money," I say with a fake smile.

Damon makes a sound of amusement in the back of his throat. "They wish."

We stare at each other. "Tell me what you know, Damon. Did Victor do it?"

He stretches his neck from side to side. "He did. I heard him talking about it with a few of the men. Between you and me? I don't know what the fuck is wrong with him, but I don't trust him."

I exhale. "Finally, someone else with some damn sense."

"And what are you going to do with this information?" he asks, crossing his arms over his chest. "Better yet, what the fuck do you want *me* to do with it?"

Victor pokes his head into my office. "What are you two talking about?"

"That's between Julianna and I," Damon replies, and Victor's whole expression changes, like his mask just drops revealing his true, angry self.

"What did you just say to me?" Victor states, getting into Damon's face.

Damon doesn't flinch, he just sits there, his eyes daring Victor to try something.

"What is going on here?" Dad asks as he enters my office. It's a fucking reunion in here.

"He's been disrespectful," Victor seethes, turning back to Dad. "I asked him what he and Julianna were in here talking about."

"And I told him that is between Julianna and myself," Damon replies, moving to stand next to me. Dad's eyes flare at Damon's obvious loyalty to me, and not to Victor.

"You would stay loyal to my daughter over Victor?" Dad asks, curiosity in his tone.

"Any day of the week."

Victor growls, and Dad pulls him back. "My daughter is a very capable woman, isn't she?" he says with pride.

"Dad, after you decided that Victor will not be president and he publicly lost in a fight to the Devils' president, what is he still doing here? And better yet, why does he have any say about anything?" I give Victor a fake smile.

"Julianna," Dad admonishes me.

"As the heir to the Angels MC, I am asking that Victor be removed from my space. Damon, will you see to it that this man is escorted out? He is making it hard for me to do my work." I put my headphones on to indicate that I do not want to be interrupted.

Damon smirks and stands, ushering Victor out. My dad tries to talk to me, but I just point to my headphones, indicating I cannot hear him.

I don't have time for bullshit. Not anymore.

Chapter Thirty

Romeo

We get the new venue for Devil's Play sorted, but it will take a week or so to set it all up again. I tell Echo to take a week of paid leave and to get some rest and relaxation in. Knowing her, though, that is the very last thing she will do. The woman is a workaholic.

I decide to drop in and talk with my grandfather. I find him sitting in front of the TV, Grandpa Johnny with a beer and my grandma, Cathy, with what looks like something a little stronger.

"Who died?" he asks, frowning and sharing a look with Cathy. "Did someone die? Why else would the president of the Devils MC be dropping in like this?"

I laugh and sit down in their worn, comfy leather couch. "No one died. Yet. I just thought I'd see how you both are doing."

"We're fine, Romeo. How are you?" Grandma asks, studying me. It's so weird to think that once upon a time she was best friends with Libby. And that Libby and Johnny were together and very much in love. If he knew that Libby still loved him, would he leave Cathy even now to get those last few years of happiness? I'm almost too scared to find out. Grandma Cathy is not the warmest person, but she *is* my grandmother.

"I'm okay. You know, besides the businesses being burned down, and tensions rising, which will likely lead to a full-blown war," I reply, forcing a smile.

Johnny's eyebrows rise. "Jesus Christ, some things never change, do they?"

If only he knew how right he was. I'm basically in the exact same position he was.

"It doesn't seem so. Dad's on vacation, and the whole place is falling apart. Who said being president was fun?"

He barks out a laugh and takes a drink, his eyes crinkling at the corners. "No one, that's who. So the Angels hit us first. I didn't think they had it in them."

"Hotheaded, low-IQ Victor seems to have gone rogue," I explain, glancing over at the photo of me as a kid on the wall. I'm at the beach and holding a big ice cream cone. A much simpler time. Cathy stays quiet, but I notice her frown. "I don't know how much Paulie knows, but he seems to turn a blind eye when it comes to Victor."

"That family all have something wrong with them," Cathy says, bitterness in her tone. Her expression has morphed into something akin to hatred. "They are all just like Libby Rose."

"Wasn't she your best friend once upon a time?" I ask, trying to be casual.

She nods. "Yes, before she broke Johnny's heart and showed her true colors."

I notice that the man in question stays silent, and doesn't offer a bad word about Libby. I want to point out that without Libby leaving Johnny, Cathy wouldn't be in the picture, but obviously I don't.

"You know I love you guys, right?" I say quietly. They might hate me when they find out about Julianna.

Johnny turns his familiar brown eyes to me and frowns. "Are you sure *you're* not dying?"

With a quick laugh I stand up and give them both a kiss on the cheek and then get out of there. As much as I want to see Julianna tonight, I decide it's probably best if I stay at the clubhouse. If any more shit goes down, I need to be right here, and I want everyone to see that I'm here and doing what I can to get justice for the shit Victor has pulled.

It's late by the time I climb into bed, and I finally check my texts.

Julianna: I miss you.

Romeo: Miss you more.

Julianna: Don't think that's possible.

Romeo: Aren't we disgustingly cute?

Julianna: Yes, we are. And Victor did start the fires.

Romeo: I knew it. We have proof?

Julianna: Damon told me, he's on my side.

I like that she has support there, but why does it have to be that good-looking motherfucker?

Julianna: Victor thinks he's still going to marry me.

Of course he does, the asshole.

Romeo: Over my cold dead body.

Julianna: I think he is willing to do anything before people find out the truth. He's spiraling. That makes him dangerous.

Romeo: It won't come to that.

River was following him around all day, but now I've put Trent on it so River can go get some rest. I thought giving the old man something to do might keep him busy, too. So far, nothing. But Victor did just commit arson, so I'm guessing he would be keeping a low profile for now. I have a few options here.

I can try to get Victor kicked out of the club, by gathering evidence and showing everyone who he truly is, or I can just take care of him myself once and for all and not bother trying to prove anything. Either way, I will be getting him far away from Julianna. He can have Veronica and they can live happily ever after for all I care. If he makes it out of here alive, that is.

But Julianna is mine.

And the Angels MC?

It's hers.

Chapter Thirty-One

Julianna

It's been a while since I've seen Rosalind, and I hadn't wondered where she was until I see her at the clubhouse. She's drinking a cocktail and it's not even eleven a.m.

"What's going on with you?" I ask, brow furrowing. She dropped by my house that day, and I haven't heard from her since.

"Nothing much. I went away for a few days with my friends, but thanks for noticing," she replies, nodding toward her beverage. "Want a mojito?"

"No thank you, it's a little early for me," I say, sitting down next to her on the couch. "What's new with you?"

"Well, I met a new guy," she replies, eyes lighting up. "Which has been good. You know what they say, to get over someone, you have to get under someone else."

"And who are you getting over?" I ask, wanting her to admit that she was sleeping with Romeo.

But instead she just waves her free hand. "Doesn't matter now. He ghosted me, and I'm moving on with my life. I heard about Veronica. Awkward."

"Not as awkward as him thinking he still has a chance of marrying me," I grumble. "You know, at the end of the day we are still sisters, and I think we should talk about—"

"Nothing to talk about," she says, shrugging. "It's fine. I know I can be a bitch, but you have always been a good sister, Julianna. I mean, you tried. This family is fucked-up, but you deserve to be happy, too."

"I think that's the nicest thing you've ever said to me," I reply, licking my suddenly dry lips. "Thank you."

We said nothing, but also everything.

The truth is I wouldn't swap my life with Johnny for anything. I never thought I'd get to experience a love like this, and now that I have, I'm going to treasure and hold on to it.

Words I never thought I'd ever hear myself say. I'm a strong, independent woman, always have been, but with Johnny? He just allows me to be in my feminine energy, but I know that no matter what comes up, he will handle it. He will do whatever he needs to protect me, and I've never felt safer with someone. I've never trusted anyone or loved anyone like I do Johnny. Fucking scary, but also simply magical.

Speak of the devil...

Johnny: Do you have a minute for a phone call? I have a real estate question for you.

Julianna: Sure, give me ten.

I'm sitting in my car when he calls, asking me about property they own that will now be the new Devil's Play, and a few other questions about their investment properties. He's very knowledgeable on the construction side of things, and I could learn more of that from him, but when it comes to real estate—that is my thing. I answer to my best ability, giving him advice that I've learned along the way and that has helped me raise the wealth of the Angels.

"Thank you," he says, and I can hear the smile in his tone. "You are so sexy and smart, you know that? I'm seriously the luckiest man alive."

He makes me feel so appreciated, and I love that he came to me for help, unlike Victor, who would never put me on his level like that. Romeo makes me feel like an equal, and that's all I wanted. After we end the call, I get a text from him a few minutes later.

Johnny: Victor was spotted on Montanna territory. Got eyes on him so will see what the hell he's up to.

I wonder what Victor is planning next. Whatever it is, it can't be good. My dad really needs to put him out of his misery and tell him his time has passed.

Julianna: Stay safe.

Johnny: Always. You too. Where are you now?

Julianna: Just heading home. I will see you tonight.

I'm about to pull out of the driveway when I see my dad walk out of the clubhouse and over to me, so I roll down my window.

"You heading home?" he asks, and I nod. "I thought we could talk about Victor and the marriage."

I arch my brow, my hands still resting on the steering wheel. "Dad, why is this even an issue? You agreed he wouldn't be president, he lost the fight to Romeo. This shouldn't even be on the table. I'm shocked you are acting like I still have to go through with this considering his relationship with Veronica. I'm sure you can understand the awkward position it's put me in. She's my sister and they are now openly flaunting their relationship. Do you think people would respect me knowing that?"

He nods slowly, leaning on my car. "They will have to respect you. There is no one else who can run this MC but him. You have to marry him, Julianna."

"Have you lost your mind? You told the Devils Victor would not be president or else we'd go to war. I am in no way marrying him." I turn the car off and get out of my car, wanting to stand face-to-face with him.

My father runs a hand through his hair. "Why must you start with this, Julianna?"

I cannot believe my father is this dense.

"Victor is the one starting everything," I remind him.

Growing up I never felt like my dad put the club in front of us kids, but in this moment I can truly see where his priorities lie. He will willingly destroy two of his daughters to fulfill our family legacy, and he will still sleep well at night.

"You don't think Victor messed up by attacking the Devils? Or do you genuinely think he's going to make a good president? Because to me it looks like he's already making things much worse and it's not even official yet. I know it was him who started those fires, Dad. Why are you so blind when it comes to him?"

His lips tighten into a line. "Victor said he didn't. I know you don't see it now, but in the long term this will be the best decision. And it will all work out. How long do you think it'll be before Veronica falls in love with someone new? How long before you settle into your new role as the president's wife? Everyone will adapt, and it will all be okay. You need to trust that I know what is best, Julianna. I've been planning this for years. I can't just change my mind because Victor isn't your knight in shining armor. It's bigger than you. We have to think about the club as a whole. The men will follow Victor, and yes, he made a mistake with starting that fight, but he's only human. He will make some mistakes along the way."

I've had it.

"I'm not marrying him!" I scream, and in this moment, I have zero control of what is coming out of my mouth. "I will take my inheritance myself. I will run the Angels."

"I will never agree—"

"You do not have a say. I have Callisto blood and you do not. I outrank you!" I shout, and in that moment my father's face clouds over in rage. And before I'm able to walk it back, he slaps me across my cheek and sticks a finger in my face.

"Don't you ever disrespect me like that again. I am the president. I will declare—"

"What does the charter say? Have you even fucking read it? I have. A *man* does not have to lead. The firstborn *child* does. If you want to come for me, come for me, but I will fight this and the men will follow me, too. You saw where Damon's loyalties were—"

"Yes, but not all of the men will feel that way. You can't protect the MC like Victor can."

"Protect the MC? How is starting a war protecting the MC?"

"I have to go, but you need to prepare yourself," he

says, walking off, and not giving me a chance to say anything further.

"He's the one who needs to prepare himself," I mutter to myself as I get back in the car and catch my breath. It's clear he doesn't care about my feelings at all, and I doubt he ever will. I need to look out for myself because my parents aren't going to. My mom has been quiet and staying out of everything, expecting me to just blindly listen to my dad. He married into this family to become president—is that why he is vouching for Victor so hard?

Maybe he sees himself in him.

I know that my grandfather didn't always trust my dad and questioned his role as president. Maybe that's why he doesn't like it when I do the same to Victor.

I know I've been raised to welcome my role and to be proud about it, but unfortunately for them they also raised a woman with her own mind and dreams, and this club will not fall apart without Victor.

In fact, it will thrive.

Dad speaks about the long term, but he can't see what I can when I look into the future. Things are going to change, and he's going to have to accept that. He did what he wanted during his reign, and now it's time for me to have that same opportunity.

And I might not be on great terms with Veronica right now, but she's still my sister and I want her to be happy. I want everyone to be happy, and I want the club to be safe and provided for.

So who really has the best interest of the Angels MC here?

Because my bet is on me. It's time to claim my birthright, with Johnny Montanna by my side.

Chapter Thirty-Two

Romeo

It's crazy how such a simple decision can change everything. I didn't think going out for a drink with my family could end any worse than getting drunk, maybe a fight breaking out.

But I was wrong.

"I don't know how I feel about you coming out for a drink," I grumble, eying Corey's bright smile. "You aren't even legal yet."

She lifts her glass. "It's a soda, Ro. I told you. I'm just going to play pool and my brother said it was fine."

I frown at Matthew. He's a good brother, the best, and he's never been able to say no to his younger siblings.

"You just don't want the bar to see me beat you in pool," she adds with a smirk, giving me a quick hug. "Come on, stop being so boring. Think about what you were doing at my age and be thankful I even want to hang out with you oldies."

My lip twitches at that, because she's right. At her age I was knee-deep in so much pussy, drugs and alcohol and was nothing like she is. "All right, then. Challenge accepted."

I beat her in both games and then Matthew takes over and plays while River and I sit at a bar with a drink.

"Things at Devil's Play going okay?" River asks, scanning the dance floor.

I nod. "Yeah, the new venue is even better. It has more space. I think we'll be up and running in no time; Echo is working hard to get everything organized. And we're claiming the old property on insurance—we want to prove that the fire was deliberately lit. The cops still won't give me the footage; I think they know some shit might go down if we see who did it."

"Are they going to do anything about it, then?" he asks, lips tightening. "Surely they won't just let him get away with this."

"They said they are looking into it," I reply with a slight shrug, placing my beer back on the bar. "I'm going to give them a little time, because it would be easier if they did figure out who it was and arrested him. But realistically we're going to have to handle this ourselves."

And preferably before my dad gets back from vacation.

I don't know how I'm going to explain that a few buildings got burned down, we got into a fight and, oh yeah, I'm also married to Julianna Callisto.

I've always been the golden child—the only child, but golden nonetheless—but I think this whole situation is going to have my dad wishing he'd kept procreating.

And that isn't a good feeling for me. However, I have to live my life the way I want to. I can't live for other people anymore.

"Sounds like Paulie has his head up his ass," River adds, turning to me. "And we need to be prepared for him not seeing reason. If he's just going to let Victor continue on being an asshole, going back on his promise to you, we're going to have to retaliate."

"I know. I'm hoping Paulie can rein him in, but I don't think he will. So shit is going to get ugly, and fast."

"Is that going to affect things with...?" He trails off, as if not even wanting to say her name out loud in case someone else hears. "You know."

"Maybe. But she knows what Victor is doing is wrong, and if we play it right we can make it work for both of us. Getting rid of Victor means that she could take over the club cleanly." I duck my head. "If they can get rid of their fucking outdated rules. Julianna is a much better leader than Victor and being a woman shouldn't stop that."

"You know what they say?"

"What?" I ask, picking my beer back up and taking a sip.

"Tradition is just peer pressure from dead people," he says, lip twitching.

I laugh out loud. "Well, she isn't going to let that stop her."

Matthew and Corey come up to us. "What time is the party tomorrow?"

"Uh, I think it starts around four p.m."

Everyone is coming to the clubhouse for dinner, drinks and celebration. We usually play music, dance, and all the children play in the yard or in our pool. It's a lot of fun, and the first party we'll be having with me as president, so it's kind of a big deal. Trent's wife, Vanessa, is helping me organize all of the food and everything, and for that I am grateful. My mom would have done it if she was here, but I had no idea where to start. Plus, including Vanessa might make Trent back off a little more, although he has been pretty quiet as of recently. Must have accepted his fate being led by me. That or he's biding his time and waiting to pounce.

"We'll be there," Matthew says. "Hey, we're going to head out."

I give Corey a hug, and him a fist bump. "All right, you okay to drive? Do you want me to take Corey home?"

"Nah, I have a lady to go to, so I can do it."

River shakes his head. "Ruled by pussy. All three of us."

"Gross," Corey says with a scrunched-up nose.

"Let me take Corey. You hang with River and help close out."

Matthew nods and I start to get ready to go, when I get a text from Julianna.

Julianna: I am DONE. We need to figure out how we're going to announce we are married and merging the Angels and Devils. Do you think your grandfather will help us? I know my grandmother will.

Romeo: Whoa, hello to you. I'm about to drive my cousin home, then I can come to you?

She doesn't seem to read my text and decides to call me. "Babe, I cannot deal with my father anymore. And don't get me started on Victor. He has my father asking me when we're getting married. What delusional world does he live in?"

"Babe, it's okay, I'm going to drop off Corey and then I'm coming straight to you." I give my cousins a sympathetic smile. Julianna keeps going.

"Oh, and by the way my father slapped me across the face when I pointed out that he had no Callisto blood in him."

I pause when I hear that. "*What?* He put his hands on you?"

Matthew can tell I'm going to go nuclear, so he pulls Corey by the arm and points to outside, indicating he's going to take Corey home.

She stays silent, possibly regretting divulging that bit of information.

I lower my tone. "I don't care if he's your father, no one puts their hands on you. You hear me?"

"Romeo—"

"He tries that again and I'll start a fucking war over it, I do not care."

She sighs. "Shit, that's Bella calling me. Let me fill her in. Will I see you soon, husband?"

I fucking love hearing her say that word. "Yeah, give me twenty minutes." River comes over just as we are ending the call, and I look to him. "Shit is going to go down, sooner than ever."

"You going to make an announcement tomorrow, at the party?"

"You know, that isn't a bad idea. I could bring Julianna. We can announce it then."

River nods. "We'll be ready."

I clap the back of his shoulder. "You heading to Bella's after this?" I ask, turning around to signal the waitress for the check.

"Most likely. You going to see Julianna?"

"Most likely," I parrot, lip twitching. "What happened to us?"

River laughs under his breath. "What can I say? When

you know, you know. And you either make it work, or you spend the rest of your life wishing you did."

My eyes widen slightly in surprise at his deep reply. And truer words were never spoken. It would be so much easier for Julianna and me to not be together, but I know that I will never find another woman like her. Not with the connection that we have. She's one of a kind, and I'd be an idiot to walk away from that kind of love that can't be replaced. And I may be many things, but an idiot isn't one of them.

"Wise words," I say, and we clink bottles.

I'm counting out some money to pay for the drinks when Corey rushes back in, fear etched on her face. "The Angels are out front in the parking lot and attacking Matthew!" she all but screams.

I throw the money down and we run outside to see Victor and three of his men standing around Matthew's motorcycle.

And Matthew is on the ground.

Not moving.

"Call an ambulance, now," I tell Corey, while River and I run up to the men.

River leans down to check on Matthew while I get right in Victor's face. He looks surprised to see me, as if he thought Matthew was here with only Corey. "You fucking pussy, four against one?"

Victor laughs, a deep, emotionless sound. "Well, your friend shouldn't have stood in the way of what I wanted."

I don't know what he's talking about, but I throw the first punch and hit him right in the nose. He falls and then I go after the other men. I don't give two shits about who they are, they are here and are guilty by association.

One of them gets me on the side of my head, but then River jumps in and it's us two against four of them. I don't mind the odds. River is a monster fighter, and he fights dirty.

Victor gets up and we both go at it, with me kneeing him in the stomach while hitting him in the face. I don't back down. I don't take it easy. All I can see is red, adrenaline pumping through me. No one hurts my family, no one.

One of the other men jumps on my back and starts hitting me in the side of the head, so I let Victor fall to the ground while I get him off me, hitting him back. I glance over to see River getting the upper hand with the other two men, so I continue to fight for my life. I wish I had my gun or another weapon. I fucking would kill them all.

Corey sits with Matthew, waiting for the ambulance to arrive, and I vaguely look back to make sure she is safe. Blood is pouring from Victor's nose, and when I hear the sirens, the distraction of the ambulance arriving has all four of them running off, while we rush back over to Matthew. There's blood on his face and he's unresponsive.

The paramedics jump out and put a collar on him. They give him oxygen and one says that he has no pulse. They start performing CPR, and I realize this is worse than I could imagine.

Corey is bawling in River's arms and I'm just standing there in shock. How did this happen?

The paramedics pronounce him dead after ten minutes of trying to get his pulse going again.

Just like that.

The police arrive. They secure the crime scene and question everyone, making a report. They then say they're going to take him to the hospital morgue so they can perform an autopsy. They can't tell us anything right now.

"It's my fault," Corey cries in my arms. "The bald man was hitting on me, and Matthew told him to leave me alone."

"It's not your fault, it's their fault," I assure her, tears falling down my cheeks. "It's not your fault at all."

It's mine. I should've been the one to bring her home. I got distracted.

I'll hate myself forever for this. But they are going to pay.

Chapter Thirty-Three

Julianna

The smile that plays on my lips instantly disappears the second I open the door and see Romeo's face. He's bleeding, and his cheek is swollen.

"Oh my God, what happened?" I ask as he steps inside and melts into my arms.

It's later than I thought he was going to come over, but I was reading a book so I didn't mind staying up late to wait for him. But he has obviously gotten into a fight, and he doesn't bother to sneak in for the first time. I lock the door and lead him to my bed, and he doesn't say anything the whole time. He just lies down and I cuddle him. When he starts crying silently, I know something really bad has happened. I just hold him and stroke his hair until he's ready to tell me what happened.

"Matthew's dead," he says finally, and my eyes close, my arms holding him even tighter.

"What happened?" I ask, and when he tells me my heart breaks. A man was killed, and the Angels are responsible.

My club. My MC.

How could they do such a thing?

For no fucking reason?

I've never felt such anger flow through me in my life. "I'm so sorry, Johnny," I whisper, my hands shaking.

Johnny has spoken to me about his cousin before, and how gentle and kind he was, and how everyone always thought he was made for something better than the MC life.

And now that life has been taken, and for no fucking good reason at all.

He eventually falls asleep, but I don't. I stay up all night wondering how the hell I'm going to fix this. I mean, I can't bring Matthew back, but something has to be done, and Victor needs to pay for his crimes.

The next morning when I wake up, Johnny has gone and I can't help but feel worried about him, and feel so bad for his loss. I get ready and drive straight to the clubhouse. I can't let anyone know that I know what happened, but I want to see how my father handles this when the news comes out.

This is his chance to do something about Victor.

This is his chance to see through him, and stop making excuses for his behavior and acts of violence.

However, when I get there, everyone is carrying on as normal, like no one knows what happened last night. Even though Victor and the other men are covered in bruises and cuts. Victor's nose looks broken, yet no one says anything. Maybe everyone knows but is trying to keep it on the down-low, because obviously they would have asked him what happened.

Why is no one saying anything about Matthew?

I want to scream.

I browse the news app on my phone to see if there's anything on there, but no, nothing.

It's like last night never happened to the rest of the world, and it makes me feel sick. I'm about to walk into my dad's office and demand justice when the cops show up.

I never thought I'd ever say this, but fucking finally.

They ask to speak to the men who were at the biker bar last night, and everyone plays dumb. But the cops show photos and video from the bar of Victor and three of our other members, Ben, Mitch and Ron. They are all close to Victor, like his little entourage, and looking back now I can see that he had been grooming them for some time to be loyal to him over anyone. He's been waiting, planning, and now he's finally executing. And my father is none the wiser.

Speaking of the devil, Dad turns to me. "Call our lawyer and tell him to meet us at the police station."

I nod and pull out my phone, watching the cops handcuff the men and put them in the back of the police van. I take my time calling the lawyer, but figure I better do it anyway. Even murderers are entitled to some legal representation.

My mom and Veronica are obviously upset, crying and carrying on, even though my dad isn't even the one in hot water. He still went with them to the police station, probably because he has no idea what Victor is capable of. He still thinks Victor was born to be a leader and is going to do something great for our MC.

Maybe he's not of sound mind.

I don't think anyone is that blind, especially for someone not of your own blood.

Julianna: Cops came and arrested them.

Johnny: Fuck. I wanted to get my hands on him myself.

Julianna: By the look of him you already did.

Johnny: Yeah, but he's still breathing.

Julianna: When am I seeing you?

Johnny: I'll be with my family tonight. Party got postponed.

Julianna: Okay, I love you. He won't get away with this.

He doesn't reply or tell me he loves me back, and I know I'm being ridiculous and he's grieving, but what if he also blames me for this? I'm an Angel, these are my members and they did this to his family. I don't know if roles were reversed if I'd feel any different than him. Some people never heal from the loss of a loved one, and I can understand why he would associate it all with me.

By the end of the day, the men are out on a very expensive bail, pending trial. They're back at the clubhouse, laughing and shooting the shit. I think Veronica just went in the back and gave Victor a blowjob. This is a sick joke. I can't keep sitting around waiting for Dad to step in, because he's clearly not going to.

The time has come for me to stand up for what I believe in.

If Victor doesn't have to do time, he needs to be taken care of.

Am I capable of that?

I don't know.

But the bastard needs to die.

Chapter Thirty-Four

Romeo

After sorting out all the details for the funeral, I stay at the clubhouse and spend time with my family. Tonight was supposed to be the first club party under my leadership, but instead we are all in mourning.

Matthew didn't deserve to die. He was honorable, and just a good person, and should have gotten married and had children. Instead his life was cut short because of Victor's power trip.

Corey told me what happened. She had walked out of the bar and the men had started whistling and carrying on, and then Victor approached and tried to grab her. I don't know if he saw Matthew first and that's why he did it, or if he was just being an asshole because he saw an attractive girl. Either way, obviously Matthew stepped in to protect his sister and then they all started attacking him. Matthew was a strong fighter, but four on one is not an even fight. Corey said that Matthew was holding his own but when they got him down, Victor grabbed his head and slammed it to the ground. Repeatedly. That wasn't a fistfight, it was a fucking murder. Victor was going in for the kill.

I was the one to tell his mom what happened.

I will never forget the look on her face.

River knocks on my bedroom door, and when I open it he lifts up a bottle of whiskey. I open my door wider and he comes in and sits on my bed, opening and drinking straight from the bottle before passing it over to me.

"You know what Matthew said to me the other day? He said I looked different. Lighter, happier. And then he smiled and said whoever she is, she's a lucky woman," River says, laughing without humor. "He saw the good in everyone. Even a bastard like me."

I take a drink and pass it back to him. "I know. Why do bad things happen to good people?"

"They say the good die young," he mutters bitterly, shaking his head. "Do we have any word on what's happening with Victor?"

"He was arrested, but Julianna said he was out on bail by this evening," I say, taking another swig after he passes it back, and staring at the bottle. "I tried to keep the peace, I really did. I didn't want this for us. But now there's no backing down. I'll do whatever I need to."

Victor is not going to hurt anyone else.

"I know you did," River comments, slapping me on the back. "But you can't fight honorably with someone who has no honor."

He's right, but I didn't want to stoop to his level. I wanted to rise above.

But now Matthew is in the ground, and that's the level I'm at.

And that's the level that Victor will end up in, too.

In the ground.

Except unlike Matthew, no one will miss his ass.

"I'm worried about Corey," I admit, brow furrowing.

"She's not doing well. I think she's traumatized from what she saw."

And fair enough. She saw her big brother take a hit and die from it. I don't know how one gets over that, especially a young impressionable girl. This will scar her forever and change the course of her life.

"We will be there for her" is all River says, but his tone shows that he too is worried about how this will affect her. I'm going to suggest that she sees someone, like a therapist, to help her get through it.

"Yes, we will." I take one more swig. "Call church. We're going to war."

It's a few nights later before I get to see Julianna, on the day of the funeral. The Angels had enough sense to stay out of our way and let us grieve in peace.

She opens the door in her robe, her arms spread out to me, and there are no words, just touch, kissing and reconnecting.

Once we get that out of the way we catch up on everything that's been happening over the last few days. I tell her about the funeral, and Corey sobbing on the casket, and she tells me how Victor has been lying low, and hasn't really left the clubhouse since he got released from custody. No one has brought up the marriage again, and time seems to be standing still for now. I'm glad things have calmed down, but it's only a matter of time until the next storm.

Kissing her temple, I pull her tight against me, enjoying the skin-on-skin contact. How I've missed this.

Just being with her feels like home.

"Johnny?"

"Yes?" I reply, kissing her neck.

"It's time. We need to announce our marriage and we need to figure out a way to get rid of Victor. Enough talking. We've been talking about this for weeks. It's time for action. This is war. Devils and Angels against Victor and his crew."

I nod, never more in love with my wife than I am right now.

"You need to round up who is loyal to you and who is loyal to Victor. I don't want to go after the ones who will stay loyal to the Callistos, but Victor may stage a mutiny and your father, no offense, is fucking clueless."

"I'm already on it. Do you think I should finally talk to Damon? Openly? Letting him know what I'm planning?" The mention of the good-looking biker annoys me. I know Julianna is my wife, but fuck, do I not like that bastard. But if he is loyal to Julianna, that's all I care about.

I nod. "Yeah, as long as he knows his place."

She smirks.

"When we have my president party, I want you and Libby to come. It's time."

Chapter Thirty-Five

Julianna

"Damon, can we speak outside for a moment? It's about the Hillsdale property."

He raises his eyes in confusion, but follows me regardless. "Julianna, I know for a fact you sold the Hillsdale property three months ago. So what's this about?" he says as soon as we're out of earshot.

"Look, Damon, I like you. I trust you. So I hope you're not going to freak out when I tell you what I'm about to tell you."

He nods.

"I am not marrying Victor. I am not marrying anyone my father chooses. Instead I am going to make a play to run the Angels myself, on my own."

Damon is not a man of many words. He just raises his eyebrows but lets me continue.

"I need support from the men. Do I have it?" I wring my hands waiting for his answer. If I do not have Damon's support, there is no way I'll have the other men's support.

"So you're not marrying anyone?" is the first thing he asks.

If I'm going to lead, I need to be honest. "I *am* married…
to Romeo Montanna."

I don't think I've ever seen a man's eyes bug out as
much as Damon's do.

"I know. We're going to unite the Devils and Angels—
I'm going to lead the Angels and he's going to lead the
Devils. As equals."

Damon starts pacing for what must be fifteen minutes. Finally he turns to me. "I'll follow you. You have
my support. And I know a few other men who will feel
the same."

For the first time, I finally feel supported by the Angels. I can do this. I know I can.

"I won't let you down."

"But not all of them will have your back," he adds.
"You'll have your work cut out for you."

"I always liked a challenge."

Chapter Thirty-Six

Romeo

Julianna asks her dad to meet us at her grandma's house.
Neutral grounds, and we sure as hell could use the support.
Her grandmother thinks it'll go over better if we tell her
father first, before announcing our marriage to the MCs.
She has a point.

We show up together, on my bike, Julianna on the
back, arms around me. Her parents stand at the front
door, mouths wide open, as the reality of the situation
must be hitting them. I park my bike behind their car,
and Julianna hops off first, removing her helmet and
staring at her parents. It's all out in the open now, there's
no going back.

Hand in hand, we walk up to the front door together.

"What the hell," her dad says, glancing between us.
"What is the meaning of this? Is this why you don't
want to marry Victor?"

"No, I still wouldn't marry Victor if he was the last
man on earth," she replies, clearing her throat. "Dad and
Mom, this is Johnny, the love of my life. Johnny, these
are my parents."

Libby comes out and wrangles us inside, while her dad takes a moment outside to compose himself.

"Do you think we're doing the right thing?" I ask Libby, feeling nervous as shit, not for me, but for Julianna. I don't want her family to cut her off or make her feel bad for loving me. I just want them to support her, and us, and I don't fucking know. I want the happy ending, is that too much to ask?

She smiles kindly and hands me a cup of coffee. "I don't think I can answer that for you. If you both feel this is right, then it's right. I'm here for you both, no matter what happens today."

"Are you okay?" I ask Julianna, and she nods. After taking a deep breath, she glances toward the door. "I'm worried about you. I don't want him to try to attack you or something. I don't know, I'm just very nervous. Did you see his face? I thought he was going to have a heart attack."

I'm worried about her; meanwhile she's worried for me.

If that isn't love, I don't know what is.

Julianna sits down, wringing her hands as her parents step into the room. "I not only don't want to marry Victor, but I can't. Johnny—uh, Romeo—I love him. We're—"

"You have to be kidding me. You're in love with Romeo?" Paulie laughs without humor. "I know Victor has his faults, but how could you do this? You have a responsibility to the Angels."

"She has nothing but loyalty for the Angels," I say, moving forward to the edge of the couch in case I have to get up. "She can love me and her club; the two aren't mutually exclusive."

"Julianna, I don't understand how you thought this would be okay," her mother adds, frowning. "You knew your responsibility."

Paulie lifts his eyes to Libby, who stares back unflinchingly. "Of course you support this, and knew about it."

"Nanny spent her whole life wishing she made a different decision—she loved Johnny Boy. I don't want to spend the rest of my life wishing I followed my heart. I want to be with someone I love, Dad, and I don't think that's asking too much," Julianna says in a calm tone.

"What are you talking about? Your grandmother left Johnny for my dad, you know what happened. We've all heard the story," her mother says, lips tightening.

"That is not what happened," Libby states, sighing, and tells them the story.

Paulie scrubs his hand down his face. "You and Julianna are in different situations. You did what you had to do in the end, and she has to do the same. I'm sorry, Julianna, but you had to have known that messing around with Romeo Montanna wasn't a good idea. You could have picked...anyone else. Anyone."

"Bullshit. You had me married off to Victor by the time I was sixteen. I never had a choice. Instead you were blinded by Victor's manipulation and you not only gave me to him on a silver platter, but you let the perv prey on your youngest daughter the minute she turned eighteen. Don't sit here and tell me I had a choice. I never had a choice and that stops now. Nanny showed me the charter. You have no fucking say. This is my birthright, and while what Poppy did with you and mom worked out for you, that was because Mom had no interest in running an MC. It was an exception, not the rule."

Her father is on his feet now. "He's the president of the Devils MC. Surely you can understand why that is never going to work. What did you think was going to happen by calling me here today and telling me this?"

"Nothing. I knew you would do nothing. Because you never do anything. You let Victor manipulate you. I'm giving you and Mom the courtesy by letting you be the first to know that Johnny and I are already married."

There is a hush in the room.

"I want to be with Romeo, and I want to lead the Angels," Julianna says, and I'm proud of the strength in her tone. She reaches out and takes my hand in hers. "There will be no war, no more fighting. No more Victor senselessly attacking innocent men. We have a plan to keep the peace."

"You make it sound like it's that easy. Do you think the men will follow a woman? They won't. You can't do as you fucking please, expecting them to blindly follow you," he growls, shaking his head.

"The men will follow me. I have some support already, and the others will come around," Julianna calmly explains.

"Who?"

She stays quiet, probably not wanting to give everything away for nothing.

He starts to pace a little and then turns back to his daughter. "There is no way this is going to work, I'm sorry. You have to marry Victor. That is the path that has been mapped out for you. I don't want to hear about this again. Both of you need to end this, now. Figure it out."

He storms out with his wife, leaving the rest of us in silence.

"Well then," Libby muses, running her hands together. "Give him some time. This would have been a shock for him."

Julianna snuggles into me and I wrap my arm around her. "We made the first big step, and he didn't try to kill me, so I guess it didn't go so bad."

"You know what, you're right. I just hope he doesn't go back and tell everyone," she says, frowning.

"He won't," Libby says, picking up her cup of tea and glancing at us over it. "It won't look good on anyone if this came out. Everything is crumbling for him right now, and he's going to try to keep it together. Or at least appear that way for the clubhouse."

"Do you want to stay here tonight?" Libby asks, arching her brow at me. "That way you can avoid any drama with Victor, and Johnny, you don't have to get into another fight just yet. Especially when we are trying to show Paulie that you are the right choice."

Julianna shrugs. "That works for me."

And so it's decided. Julianna stays put, while I head over to my grandparents' house and face the music. When I get there, my grandpa is sitting and watching a movie while my grandma is in her bedroom, so I take this opportunity to come and speak to him alone.

"Twice in one week," he comments, giving the side-eye. "You going to tell me what's really going on?"

"Only if you don't have a heart attack on me," I tease, and he smirks.

"You're not that lucky. Now tell me what's going on," he says, pausing the movie and giving me his full attention.

"Where do I even start—"

"From the beginning—"

And for the second time today, I share the story of this stupid love grudge that our families have and the truth behind it.

He rubs the back of his neck. "Fuck, maybe I will have a heart attack. Libby told you that?"

I nod. "She said you were her soulmate. The one who got away, and all of that."

"I didn't think at my age I could be genuinely surprised," he says, brow furrowing. "God, Libby, why didn't you just come to me and tell me what my dad was doing?" He looks up at me, as if only just remembering I'm still here. "I knew he didn't like her, but I never thought he would do something like that. And you know what the most messed-up thing is? After she ran off with Mikey, Dad said, 'I told you she was bad news.' When he was the one who chased her off! That bastard. If he wasn't already dead…"

I wait for him to process this and then bring it back to me. "And you. Julianna Callisto? You really are my grandson, aren't you? What are you going to do? Your father is going to be pissed."

"I know," I admit, sighing. "But I love her, and I want to be with her. What else can I do? I don't want to live my life without her. I will fight for the woman I love. The Devils and Angels can merge back together—"

My grandma walks out, her face red with anger, and I have to wonder how long she'd been around the corner listening. "Romeo Montanna, are you crazy? You want to throw everything away over a woman? There are billions of women out there, billions. It's not worth it. She's not worth it. And I'm not going to let you walk away from your family legacy for a bit of forbidden action."

Her tone sounds personal, like this isn't really about

me as much as Grandpa and Libby, but I'm not going to anger her any further.

"I know it's upsetting, but this is my life, and I will live it how I choose. I love you both very much, and I was hoping you could support me, like Libby is supporting Julianna. It would be nice to have someone in my corner," I say gently, thinking Grandpa might understand where I'm coming from. He's been there, and I'm sure that he would have fought for Libby Rose if he knew the situation she was in. The look on his face when I told him said it all.

She was his soulmate too.

I know my grandma is upset by this, and it's understandable. No one wants to feel second best, even after all of these years they've spent together. And to know that her husband might not have chosen her if he could go back must hurt.

But it's the truth.

That doesn't mean that they don't love each other, though. They've had a beautiful life together and continued the family empire, something I might not be doing.

"Johnny, tell him," Grandma says, scowling. Her fingers are trembling when she points at me. "Don't let him throw his life away over a Callisto! Bad blood, all of them."

"Cathy," he chastises gently, gesturing for her to sit down. "He's right, it's his life. Who am I to tell him not to be with the person he loves? True love is rare, and it should be cherished, not ignored just because it doesn't go according to someone else's plan. Romeo can marry who he wants. I know that Julianna, however, doesn't have the same option. Have you told your dad?"

I shake my head. "He's back tomorrow, so I will speak to him and Mom then."

Grandma sits down as told, but she looks really angry. In fact, I don't think I've ever seen her like this before. Good thing I didn't tell her I was already married. She appears unsettled, and it's clear that she has held on to this grudge against Libby and her family for a long time. It must be draining to feel this way about an old friend, and I hope one day she can let it go and find peace over the situation. "I don't think you should tell anyone else about this."

"He should tell his father as a family courtesy." Grandpa frowns, shaking his head at her. "You need to take yourself out of the equation and make this about Romeo." Ouch.

Not wanting to stay around for an elderly married argument, I hightail it out of there thinking about everything that's been said today.

Some surprise, some empathy, but mostly a lot of what the fuck.

Now I just need to speak with Dad and see what happens next.

Chapter Thirty-Seven

Julianna

When my mom calls the next day and asks me to join them at the clubhouse for dinner, Nanny comes with me. When no one says anything to me about Johnny, I figure they are yet to say anything to the MC, especially when my sisters don't bring anything up. I know that Rosalind would have had something to say about me being with Johnny, not that I would have cared at this stage.

"Where's Victor?" I ask Veronica as we're sitting around the dinner table, wondering if he's going to try to speak to me now that I'm here. I feel safer knowing I'm not alone, though, and my grandma won't be leaving my side.

"I don't know—we broke up," she says, shrugging. The fact that she's acting like it doesn't bother her when she's been so dramatic about him all this time makes me think that she's not telling the truth.

"Why?" I ask, frowning.

She purses her lips, tapping her long French-tipped nails on the table. "There's just a lot going on right now, so we decided to take a break. He has to marry you, after all—Dad won't budge on letting me take your place, and Victor wants to be president. So he will do what he needs to to get there."

"Even Julianna," Rosalind snickers, then attempts to straighten her face. "I'm sorry, but come on, it was funny."

I roll my eyes. "I'm not marrying Victor. I don't know how many times I have to say it."

Veronica pouts. "You're living my dream and you don't even want it. It's so unfair. Do you know what I would give to be able to marry Victor and be the president's old lady? Anything. I would give anything."

"Well, you aren't the chosen one," Rosalind reminds her, scrolling on her phone. "So let it go. Firstborn gets to take over. We just get to be rich and potentially married off to allies. It won't be so bad."

"But Victor…"

"What part of Victor will not be president do you not understand, Veronica?" I state. "This is not his. It never was. It is mine. Not yours. Not Dad's. Mine. So get over it. You can have Victor, but he will not be president."

Various plates appear on the table at my mother's hands: steak, salad, broccolini and baked potatoes.

"Thank you," I say, stiffening as Dad enters the kitchen and sits down next to my mother.

"Nice to have everyone together for a family dinner," he says, glancing around the table. "Victor was going to join us, but he has some important club business to attend to instead."

Of course Victor was invited even though he is not immediate family or even related to us at all.

"Is he going to kill someone else?" I ask, addressing the elephant that has been in this clubhouse for a long time now.

The gasp that follows would be funny if it wasn't about the death of Johnny's well-loved cousin.

"He did not kill that man on purpose," Veronica states, further proving my point that they did not break up. "It was self-defense—they got into a fight. Victor just happened to be stronger."

Dad nods. "The cops let them out on bail, which means they are innocent."

"You both are utterly delusional. I don't think that's how it works—"

"Can we just have one nice family meal, please?" Mom says, sighing and playing around with the food on her plate. "No MC politics, please. Let's just enjoy each other's company."

"Victor did kill that man. Witnesses saw it—"

"I'm sure we know who your witness was, and sorry if we aren't going to blindly believe him over our own men," Dad grits out.

"It's the truth. Have you seen the surveillance footage yet?"

Nanny shoots me a look that clearly says now is not the time so I let it go, knowing that Victor is going to get what is coming to him. I enjoy my medium-rare steak, even though anyone who knows me knows I like mine well done. My mom made it, and she doesn't know me at all.

The conversation continues with subjects such as my sisters' studies, how Nanny is doing back at her old house and the weather.

Now more than ever I know that I'm making the right choice.

I belong with someone who truly loves me.

Even though Victor is missing in action, I still sleep

at Nanny's that night. We watch movies and she braids my hair just like she used to when I was a child. It's always been her home that was calm and secure, and I realize that now.

Romeo texts me all night making sure I'm okay and we just shoot the shit with each other.

Romeo: What did you have for dinner?

Julianna: Steak.

Romeo: Well done? You know I judge you for that, right?

Even he remembered.

The next morning I go back to my house and think about what I'm going to say to my dad. I don't want to push him over the edge, but I want him to know that I'm serious about this.

When there's a knock at the door I freeze, my first thought being that Victor has shown up again, and now I'm wishing I never dropped out of those self-defense classes I used to do. But instead it's Romeo and River standing there.

"Good morning," he says with a wide grin. He has a bunch of sunflowers and he hands them to me. "For you."

"Thank you," I reply, smiling at how sweet he is.

"I thought I'd get River to set you up a new security system, if you don't mind. Or at least check out the one you have now," he explains, stepping inside. "But by the looks of the cameras outside, you're going to need an upgrade."

"Okay," I agree, giving him a kiss. "Is River your resident tech expert?"

"There's not much I can't do," River replies, winking at me.

He gets to work while Romeo and I head into the kitchen. I put the flowers in a vase and put the coffee machine on. "So you really meant it, huh?"

"Meant what?" he asks.

"No more hiding. Coming over in broad daylight when anyone could see," I reply, jumping up on the counter to sit.

He comes and stands between my legs, his hands on my hips. "Yep, I meant it. I don't care who sees me loving you. If anyone has something to say about it, they can go and get fucked."

Amused, I hold on to the back of his neck and push my body forward, kissing him. I love that we are at this stage where we aren't exactly hiding, but we still need to be careful. People aren't going to like this. And because of that we could become targets to their anger.

It's a dangerous game we're playing.

I just hope we can win.

Chapter Thirty-Eight

Romeo

"I've been thinking about it and I think I have to agree with your grandma," Grandpa Johnny says, pulling his glasses down to rub his eyes.

After leaving Julianna's with her newly installed security system, I saw a missed call from him, so I came over to make sure everything was okay. Little did I know he was just wanting to tell me he doesn't think I should be with Julianna. That's very disappointing coming from him, because I saw the look in his eyes when I told him the truth about Libby.

Hope.

He would be with Libby if he could, but he's siding with his wife, and I get that.

Maybe I shouldn't have come here for support after all.

"So that's it?" I ask, tapping my fingers on the table. "I should leave Julianna and just do as I'm told, and hope I meet another woman I'm going to love as much? Just like you did?"

Grandma is probably around the corner listening

again. I understand this must bring back a lot for her, but can't he have his own opinion?

"You could lose everything" is all he says.

"Nothing will mean anything without her," I fire back, scowling. "I thought you would understand. You've been where I am right now, except your choice was taken away from you. And now you're trying to do that for me."

"Well, I got over it and moved on, and so can you," he says, and I nod, getting the message loud and clear.

And then my dad walks in, and I realize it's a fucking intervention. He must have only just gotten back home, and they've already called him and likely told him everything.

Just fucking great.

I stand and open my mouth to speak, but he lifts his hand. "I know everything, I've been all caught up."

"I bet you have."

"Sit down," he says, taking a seat himself. His skin has gotten tanned, evidence from his tropical vacation, but his face is stern and unimpressed. And I feel like a little child again about to be scolded for something or another. "Let's talk about it."

"Okay, but nothing you say is going to make me change my mind," I state, unflinchingly.

"What if the men won't follow you? What if they don't want the Angels and Devils united?" He scoffs, shaking his head. "This club is your life, it's always been your life, and it's your family legacy. You're bluffing."

"This club is my life and I love it and all the people in it, but I'm not bluffing. This isn't some passing infatuation. I'm a man, I've been with many, many women, and I know that she is the one. I'm not going to give that up for anything. And why wouldn't the men follow me? The Angels have an almost $100 million real estate portfolio that will line everyone's pockets. Where is the downside?"

Apprehension flashes in his brown eyes. Maybe he doesn't know what to think.

"This isn't lust," I carry on. "And trust me, I know the difference. Dad, I love her. I want to have children with her. And I want you to all support me and help me figure this out instead of turning on me."

They're all acting like I did something terrible, but I'm just a man who fell in love with a beautiful woman who is perfect for him.

Fucking sue me.

"I'm sure you can see why we are all concerned. You just became president, and you have your hands pretty fucking full right now. In fact, your cousin was just killed by her family!" he yells, finally unable to keep control of his anger. He tried, I'll give him that. And that last point is a good one.

"The man who killed Matthew is not her family, he's an asshole who will be handled. Julianna is not a reflection of any of that. She is a good woman. She is smart and loyal and—"

He laughs without humor. "How loyal can she be? She's clearly not loyal to her club if she's out sleeping with you when she's meant to be marrying another man."

My hand clenches to a fist. "Do not say another word about her. I'm not going to have anyone disrespecting her—"

"We are your family, Romeo!" he grits out, rubbing the back of his neck. "I am shocked that you out of all people are willing to turn your back on us over a girl—"

"She's not just any girl. Would you choose the club over Mom if she walked away?" I ask, and of course he deflects.

"This isn't about me. You are president now, my time is over with. You are the one with that responsibility."

"Yes, I am. And that means that I can choose who I will spend the rest of my life with. You just said that I'm president, and I will lead this club, with Julianna by my side," I reply, keeping my voice calm now.

"Not that woman," he growls, looking at his own father for help. "You agree, don't you? You've been in a similar situation, and you walked away and have led a beautiful life. There are other women, Romeo."

"I don't want another woman," I say between clenched teeth. "Stop telling me what to think. I love Julianna, and that is it. I'm done with this conversation or coup or whatever the fuck this is."

"She's already putting you against your own family," Grandma says as she enters the room. I knew that she had to be lurking around somewhere. "Listen to yourself, Romeo. You've never been like this before—she has to be behind it."

It suddenly hits me how toxic they are being right now. No one is listening to understand. They just want to win and get me to do whatever they want.

"I'd like to leave you with one thing and then I'll go. We're already married," I say, and storm out of there.

I don't need this.

I ride straight to Devil's Play to check out the new place, needing a distraction. Echo is there, hanging up pictures in the lobby. "Hey." She smiles when she sees me. "What do you think? We're almost ready to reopen, we just need to hire the dancers. The auditions are to-morrow, remember?"

Ah, fuck. "Do I need to be there? I kind of have a lot going on right now," I admit, wincing at how that makes me sound.

She studies me, then moves closer. "If you don't want to, that's okay. Just send someone else down because I don't want to do it alone."

Fuck.

No, this is my damn business and I have to be here. "What time?" I ask.

"Twelve is good," she replies, picking up her clip-board and going through the papers. "Should take about two hours or so."

"I'll be there," I reply, then head to check out the bar.

A stiff drink is exactly what I need right now.

Everything has gone to hell, and now Julianna is going to be pissed that I'm looking at dancers.

My family is right, though, I have changed. Old me wouldn't have given a shit what a woman thought of anything I was doing. But they should realize that I'm actually becoming a better person. I genuinely don't want to fuck anyone else. I used to have threesomes and shit like that all the time, but the thought of shar-ing Julianna, even with another woman, makes me see red. I don't want anyone else to know her like I do, to see her beautiful naked body and how sexy she is in the bedroom. I sure as fuck don't want anyone to hear the sounds she makes and the way she arches her back...

Fuck.

And now I'm hard at a burlesque bar.

Wonderful.

One drink and I'm out of there.

Chapter Thirty-Nine

Julianna

That evening I meet up with Bella and we go for a walk. I love being outside, the breeze grounding me. And a walk with good conversation with your best friend makes it ten times better.

We have dinner at a little café and then go our separate ways. I stop to put gas in the car and am surprised when I see a familiar bike riding past. Curious, I decide to follow him. I'm on the other side of town from the clubhouse, so I don't know what Victor would be doing, but I'm going to find out.

Staying several cars behind, I follow for about forty-five minutes until he stops at a small house. I decide to park my car back down the road and walk through the brush to hide behind a bush and watch. Johnny would kill me if he could see me right now. In fact, just in case something happens to me, I send him a text sharing my location.

Crouched behind the bush, I'm glad I'm in all black and not hot pink or something because he definitely would have been able to see me. Staying still, I watch as Victor gets off his bike. The front door to the cabin opens and an older woman comes out. I've seen this woman, somewhere, but a name doesn't come to mind straight away.

She hugs Victor warmly, which makes me think they are family. I don't think they are romantically involved as she is gray and older, unless he's into that kind of thing.

I wonder if she's Victor's mom or something, but both of his parents have passed, or at least that's what he's told everyone. I take a couple of photos of them, in case I need them for evidence. They exchange a few words and then they both disappear inside, and I rush back to my car and drive back home.

It's only when I pull up to my house and get out of the car I realize where I've seen the woman before.

Goose bumps appear over my skin as the revelation hits me.

Johnny calls me, panicking after only just seeing my text. "Are you okay? Why the hell were you out there?"

"I'm okay. Can you come over? I have something I need to show you," I say, opening my front door and going inside. I set the security system with a press of my code.

"Yeah, I'll be there in twenty," he replies.

When he arrives he looks concerned, and to be honest I don't know what to say to him about what I saw, so I just show him the photo.

Of Victor embracing his grandma, Cathy.

"What the fuck?" is all he can manage to get out.

I quickly explain. "I went for a walk with Bella, and I saw his bike, so I followed him to a small house where he met with your grandma. I don't know what the hell is going on, and I didn't even realize who it was at first, but then I remembered where I recognized her from. The photo in your living room."

"Why the hell would she be meeting up with Victor and hugging him?" he asks, brow furrowing.

"I don't know," I admit, shrugging. "I'm not sure how this fits in with anything. Does she own a small house out there?"

"Not that I know of," he murmurs, sending the picture to himself. "I'm so angry right now. She sat there this morning and told me about how there are plenty of women out there and I should prioritize the club. Meanwhile she's out hugging the man who killed Matthew? I feel like I don't even know this woman anymore."

"I'm sorry," I say, rubbing his back. "I was as surprised as you—it doesn't make any sense. What should we do with this?"

"I want to confront her and ask for an explanation," he says, frowning. "Is she feeding him information? He must know everything, even about us now."

I never thought about that, but he's right. "Did you tell them we're married?"

He looks devastated. "Yes, just as I was leaving."

I guess it's all out in the air now.

No skeletons left.

"I'm about to meet with the MC now to discuss recent events, so I'm not going to say anything just yet. Our first priority is to go after Victor," he says finally, sliding his phone away and pulling me into his arms. "I don't like you going off alone and rogue."

"I knew you wouldn't, but I also felt like he was doing something shady, so I wanted to know what that was," I admit. "But I'm glad I did."

He pulls a leaf out of my hair and laughs. "Next time call me for backup, please."

After a long, slow kiss he rides off to the clubhouse for his meeting and I call my grandmother, wanting to update her on the new revelation.

They were once best friends, after all, and who knows someone better than a bestie?

Chapter Forty

Romeo

I'm not going to lie, it's hard seeing my dad after our conversation this morning. I'm angry, and disappointed that he has zero care for my feelings, but I guess the club always comes first, right? Even before your own blood. I try to put my personal feelings aside and focus on the reason why we are all here.

"We lost Matthew," I start, and everyone goes silent. "And there needs to be some retribution for that. We also don't want to lose anyone else, so we all need to be on alert. Victor is unpredictable and desperate. We need to expect anything, and trust no one until the threat is out of the way."

"What are we going to do? I think we need to get rid of him before he marries the Callisto and becomes president. He will be harder to get after that," Trent states gruffly, glancing around the table.

Amusement hits me at the casual mention about getting rid of him and the fact that no one bats an eyelash at it.

"They'll know it's us and the war will just keep

going," my dad points out. "But our chances for things getting better with Victor around are nil."

"I agree with everything said," I say, looking to River at my right side. "Things will get worse before they get better, but Victor needs to go. Now that I know we're all on the same page, I'll think about how to go about it. Anything else we need to discuss?"

I stare at my dad as I say the last line, wondering if he's going to bring Julianna up or not, but he stays quiet. He's a smart man, and I think he knows that if he gives me any reason to walk, I will.

"Just one thing," River says, a smirk playing on his lips.

"What?" I ask a little reluctantly.

He glances at his watch. "Don't you have to be at Devil's Play picking out new performers right now?"

Oh fuck.

We discuss a few other matters, including our finances, and other businesses, and then end the meeting and I go to see Echo. I forgot to tell Julianna that I was going here, and I know that sounds like a cop-out, but I genuinely did forget.

Romeo: Forgot to tell you today is the day we hire the dancers.

Julianna: So you get to watch beautiful half-naked women dancing all day?

I don't really know how to reply to that, so I decide to go with honesty.

Romeo: Yes, but it doesn't mean anything and I'm coming home to you. You have nothing to worry about.

Julianna:...

Romeo: Love you.

After sitting on the news about my grandma overnight, I decide to confront her about the photograph and her connection to our enemy. I disguise this little meeting by inviting my grandparents and parents over for dinner at my house. What they don't know is that Julianna and Libby Rose are coming, too. And this whole thing is a good distraction from the sexy dancers.

I know.

Am I the drama?

It's time that the truth came out, and whatever happens, happens.

Julianna and Libby Rose are already seated at the table when all four of them arrive. My gaze ends up on Grandpa Johnny's face, because his expression is hard to deny. His eyes are full of love, regret and surprise.

"I...uh...didn't realize we were having other guests," he says, clearing his throat. "Libby, it's been a long time. I mean, I saw a glimpse of you at Mikey's funeral..."

"What is she doing here?" Grandma sneers, pointing. "You've taken it too far this time, Romeo."

My dad looks like he wants to murder me with his bare hands, but he can get in line, and my mom looks extremely confused.

Oh right, no one has told her anything yet.

"Please, everyone sit. I have an announcement to make, and everyone here has to hear it," I say, staring them down until they sit. My grandma is the last to do so.

"I don't understand why the Callistos are here," my mom says, sounding angry and confused.

"We're married and this cannot go unrecognized anymore," I explain, smiling at her.

Cathy's eyes widen in shock. "What? That's why we're here?" Her eyes narrow on her former best friend. "If you are going to announce a marriage into that family, then you are dead to me. You'll be dead to us all."

Grandpa Johnny gasps from next to her. "Now, don't say things you will regret, Cathy."

"I'm glad you are so outraged, Grandma," I say, picking up the upside-down image on the table. I printed out the photo for maximum effect. Julianna said I was being dramatic, but I'm pissed.

Grandma is the biggest hypocrite ever. And she's about to be exposed.

"And why is that?" she asks, lifting her nose.

I turn the photograph around. "Because I'm outraged too, and wondering why you are secretly meeting and embracing the man who killed Matthew. The man who has been trying to become president of the Angels and marry Julianna."

Everyone gasps, except Julianna and Libby, who knew this was coming.

My poor mom, I don't know how much more shock she'll be able to take for one night.

Grandpa Johnny takes the photo and examines it. "What is this, Cathy?" he asks, frowning.

"It's a fake photo!" she shouts, trying to gaslight everyone. "They are trying to turn it around on me just because I don't agree with them being together."

"We have multiple photos, and they are timed and dated, so maybe instead of lying you can explain to us how you even know Victor. These were taken just yesterday; I'm sure you can see by her clothing, Grandpa, or perhaps a time yesterday evening when she went missing from the house."

"She went to her book club," he replies, brow furrowing as he turns to his wife. "What is the meaning of this, Cathy?"

Her lower lip trembles as she considers her answer.

"Mom?" my dad growls. "Explain now."

"Victor is my grandson," she finally says, now crying. "I had his father when I was seventeen, but gave him up for adoption. He then died later on, in a car crash with his wife, but he had a son, Victor. I didn't tell you, Johnny, I'm sorry. I was ashamed I got pregnant before marriage, and I was told to keep it a secret."

"What?" my dad whispers, eyes wide in shock. "He's our enemy."

Victor and I have the same grandmother.

I let that sink in.

"He killed Matthew," I say once more. "Yet you judge me for wanting to be with Julianna?"

"Were you feeding him information?" Libby asks, finally speaking up. "Because it did seem like Victor was always one step ahead. And I bet he already knows about Julianna and Romeo. What plan did you both have?"

Cathy stops with the tears and purses her lips at Libby. "Oh, you must love this. I don't even know why you are here."

"I'm here to support my granddaughter," Libby fires back. "Something none of you would know about. I will be there for Julianna no matter what because I love her and want her to be happy. Shame you couldn't offer the same to Romeo."

They all go silent for a few seconds.

"We want what's best for him," Dad finally says, and I notice that my mom is staring at Julianna.

"Do you love my son?" she asks her.

"More than anything," Julianna replies without hesitation. "None of us saw this coming, but there's no one else I'd rather be with. I love him so much."

Cathy scoffs, shaking her head.

"Is that why you didn't want me to be with Romeo?" Julianna asks, frowning. "With all due respect, ma'am, your grandsons are polar opposites. Romeo is a gentleman and Victor is a monster."

Cathy slams her hands down on the table. "No one will accept you with Romeo. You don't have a choice."

Mom stands up and everyone goes silent. "I support them. If she's who my son loves, then I want him to be happy."

My eyes widen in surprise at her standing up for me, but I do appreciate it.

Dad rubs his face with his hands. "Romeo can't be the president of both clubs. One of them has to walk away."

"I can lead the Angels," Julianna says quietly, glancing around the table. "I know I will have to work hard for them to accept a woman, but I already have support from some of them and I am assured more will follow. They know me and the value I bring to the MC. And I have Johnny at my back if they ever decide otherwise. We can both work together. There will be no more wars or violence."

Dad suddenly looks ill. "God protect us all."

Is that him finally accepting the situation?

"Kings and queens have ruled together for ages. If they can do it, we can do it. There never was supposed to be an Angels. But I'm glad that there is or else I never would've met Julianna," I say.

"I want a divorce," Granddad Johnny suddenly announces to Cathy. "I can't be with you anymore. I never should have been with you to begin with. I can't be with someone who had a hand in murdering my grandson." He looks over at Libby. "I'm sorry my father threatened you. I wish you would have come to me, then things might have been different."

Libby's eyes well up with tears.

Cathy starts yelling, finally showing her true colors. "Your father knew I was the right choice for you. Who do you think helped me give my son up for adoption? She would never have been able to guide the Devils and your father knew that. Hell, she had all girls. She couldn't even bear a son," she says as she points at Libby.

"Mom." My dad clears his throat. "That's not how genetics work..."

Grandma stares at him. "You are weak. Victor is not weak. You'll all be sorry."

That's the thing about a snake.

No matter how much it sheds its skin, at the end of the day...

It's still a fucking snake.

Chapter Forty-One

Julianna

With everything laid on the table and nowhere to go, the air in the room gets thick with anger, grudges long held and awkwardness.

"You should leave," Grandpa Johnny tells Cathy. "You have betrayed all of us."

"This is my family!" she screams.

"Not anymore," he whispers in a deathly calm tone. "Maybe you can go and live with Victor, since you chose him over every single one of us."

Cathy scans the room, but finds no support, so she leaves the home, slamming the door behind her. Johnny takes my hand and holds it.

"We should leave," my mom says, putting her napkin on the table and standing up. "I think that's enough for one night."

Everyone follows suit, until it's just me, Johnny and his grandfather left.

"You okay?" Johnny asks him.

"I will be," he replies, smiling sadly. "It's hard knowing what I know now, because I would have done things so differently."

I start cleaning up while Johnny takes his grandpa home, since Cathy took the car when she left.

"Are you staying here?" he asks, kissing me before he leaves.

"I'll tidy up and then head home."

"I'll meet you there," he says.

Once the house looks like it did before this traumatic night, I drive back to mine, still thinking about the dinner.

I can't believe Cathy would do that to her own family, siding with Victor over everyone and the life she had built. I don't understand her loyalty to him, and I guess I never will.

I get out of my car and walk to the door with my keys in my hand when someone grabs me by the neck, scaring the shit out of me, and throws me to the ground without warning. I hit the pavement, hard. I'm not going to lie, it fucking hurts, pain spreading through me.

"You stupid bitch!" Victor yells, kicking me in the back. "You ruined everything for me, and for my grandma. I always knew you were going to be a fucking pain in the ass."

I've never been hit by a man before, besides being slapped by my dad, and I'm not going to lie, it's brutal. His kicks are strong and filled with a powerful hate. They feel like they go on forever.

And in this moment, I've never despised anyone more.

I cover my face with my hands, preparing for the next kick, but luckily it never comes. Instead I hear the rumbling of a familiar motorcycle, and all I feel is relief as Victor steps away from me, facing Romeo's bike.

Romeo jumps off and runs toward Victor, pulling

him farther away from me and pummeling the shit out of him. He has one hand on his shirt, and the other in a fist of fury, hitting him in the face over and over again. I manage to sit up and scoot backward to my front door. Touching my face, my hand comes away with a lot of blood.

That bastard.

He's such a coward and should take responsibility for how things have panned out for him.

Romeo continues to beat the shit out of him until Victor stops moving. He then pulls out his phone and makes a call, while rushing over to check on me.

"Oh my God," Romeo whispers when he sees me up close, gently lifting me into his arms. "I can't believe that piece of shit did this to you. I'm going to go and kick his ass again. Are you okay? Is anything broken?"

"Maybe my ribs," I say, resting against him. "If you didn't arrive when you did…"

"Don't think about that, I'm here now."

A gray van pulls up and two men exit: River and Jeremiah.

Johnny gets me safely inside my car, then closes the door and has a quiet conversation with River before getting in the driver's seat and taking me to the hospital. As we drive off I see the men pick Victor up and load him in. I know he's alive, because I see his leg move. Whatever they are going to do with him, they don't want my new security cameras recording it.

"What are you going to do with him?" I ask, wincing as I try to adjust my position.

He stays silent, letting me know it's not good. They are going to kill him.

And deep down I knew that, and while I'm not a fan of murder, I can understand why.

An eye for an eye, but make it personal.

Romeo carries me into the hospital, and although it might look romantic I really am in a lot of pain. He is so sweet and attentive, though, and every time I wince, he does the same like it hurts him to see me like that. They take me in straight away, and sure enough, a few broken ribs, a head wound and some deeply grazed skin. After some pain medication and my ribs are all wrapped up, they send me on my merry way with rest the only fix.

I'm a little more than surprised when instead of taking me back home, Romeo does something that requires a lot of balls.

He takes me back into his clubhouse and walks me right in there, carrying me in his arms, like we do this every day.

"Romeo, what—oh fuck," Jeremiah says, examining me like I'm some kind of alien. "Did you kidnap the Callisto heir in revenge? Because that's a little next level."

I laugh, which hurts my ribs even more, so then I start groaning.

"Stop making her laugh," Romeo scolds, stopping at a door that I assume leads to his room. Once we're inside, he tucks me into his bed, as gentle as a man can be.

"What can I get you? Something to eat? Drink?" he asks, brushing my hair off my forehead.

"Just some water would be good, I feel a little dehydrated," I admit, and he quickly goes to his room bar fridge and gets out two bottles, opening one for me and handing it to me. The other, he places on the table next to me.

There's a sudden knock on the door and a man asks, "Did we really kidnap Julianna Callisto?"

Romeo looks like he's about to snap.

"Go and tell them I'm here of my own free will. I'm going to rest a little."

He kisses my forehead and then leaves the room, gently closing the door. I snuggle into his warm quilt, and nosily glance around his room. It's perfectly tidy and mostly decorated in black and white, with a massive TV, and sliding mirrors.

I'm surprised he brought me here, but it shows what I've known for a while now.

We are all in.

Chapter Forty-Two

Romeo

When Julianna is fast asleep, and with Jeremiah watching over her, I meet up with River in an old warehouse we own and use to store building materials. Victor is sitting on the concrete ground, his back to the wall, dried blood on his face, while River sits opposite him, a gun loosely held in his hand. Victor is a threat to the woman I love, and there's no way in hell he is going to get to walk out of here. He had his chance, and he made the wrong decision.

"You can't kill me without starting a war," Victor seethes, as if reading my mind.

River laughs without humor, as he stands up and steps back. "I think you need to worry about yourself right now."

"You will never be able to marry Julianna," Victor states, standing and facing me. "You think they'll let a Devil marry an Angel? You're wasting your time and she's not worth it anyway—"

At this point, I've had enough.

I punch him in the stomach, and give him another hit to the face.

"News flash, asshole. We're already married."

His eyes bulge like he can't believe Julianna and I had the balls to go through with it. But fuck him. Fuck everyone. We are ride or die.

Victor tries to fight back, and we go back and forth for a while until he falls down to his knees and can't get up. I think he realizes his time is over when he stops trying to.

"We share the same grandmother. We're blood." For the first time since I've known this motherfucker, he looks and sounds scared.

"You lost your chance to beg for mercy the minute you laid a hand on my cousin."

River steps up with his gun and points it at Victor's temple. He has an eerie sense of calm as he stares at him. Victor is mumbling, but he has the decency to look River in the eye. River glances over at me briefly and I nod. Normally this is something I would do, since it is my woman and my club. But I wanted to give this to River. Matthew was his brother.

"You know I'm never going to see my brother again and it's because of you," River starts, and I'm actually surprised. He's normally unemotional, but I can see why this means more to him. "Even in the afterlife, he's probably somewhere good and pure. But me, I'm not going where he is." He pushes on Victor's temple with the gun. "The only comfort I have is that wherever you're going, I will see you there. And when I die and end up where you are, I'm going to make your afterlife a living fucking hell."

And with that he shoots, and then there is nothing but blood and silence.

I should feel guilt, but I don't, and I know River

doesn't either. If anything, I see a dark satisfaction on his face as he stares down at Victor's dead body.

"I'll call the cleanup crew," River says casually, like we are chatting over lunch or something. He pulls out his phone to make the call.

And I feel a peace knowing that Julianna's world is now a much simpler place.

A lot can change in a month.

Julianna's ribs recovered, and she fought with her father tooth and nail to let her run the club with me at her side. He doesn't love it, but I think he knew he had no choice, because we weren't going to back down. He didn't want me and the Devils as his enemy, and I told him if he doesn't agree to Julianna's wishes, he will be getting just that.

Never once did I think our clubs would unite, nor did I ever think I'd be at the side of a woman, but I believe in her.

In us.

And together we are the perfect balance of beauty, brains and muscle.

She brings more to the table than I do, but having a penis has perks in our world, and we work as a perfect team.

Damon and a few of the other Angels stood up for her, and swore their loyalty. Without Damon's support, I don't think she could have done it. So I owe that pretty bastard one.

The women, Bella, Libby and even her mother and Rosalind, also stood behind her. Not without a lot of drama, but they got there in the end. To see them all standing by her side in a show of support was a very powerful moment for Julianna. Veronica is still heartbroken over Victor and hasn't been seen much since. She's staying with her mom and licking her wounds. And after seeing Paulie's bad leadership and decision-making, the Angels are turning away from him. Once you lose respect in our world, it's hard to get it back.

My men are still coming around with having a Callisto with their president, years of prejudice against them hard to go up against. They are always nice to her, of course, but still a little standoffish.

River, however, treats her like the sister he never wanted but now loves anyway. Jeremiah loves her. And she and Corey hit it off like they've known each other for years, even with the age difference. She held no grudge against Julianna for what Victor did to Matthew, which did concern me a little when they first met.

Corey is doing okay, but the loss of her brother changed her. It would change any of us. She's a little darker now, her light a little dimmed.

She doesn't smile as much and just doesn't have that spring in her step that she used to. She used to be very bubbly, and I loved that about her.

But it will come back, I know it.

I'll love her no matter what.

When I get back from a group ride, I find Julianna in the Devils' clubhouse kitchen, cooking up a storm for all the men.

"Something smells good," I say, closing my eyes for a second. "What are you making?"

"River asked for a taco night, so I'm delivering," she replies, turning around and smiling. Her cheeks are slightly flushed, and her hair is tied up in a loose knot at the top of her head. "How was your ride?"

"Good," I say, kissing her lips. "Do you need help with anything?"

She shakes her head. "No, I'm all done. I just need to make the guacamole, so tell everyone dinner will be ready in five."

"Hey."

We both turn in surprise to see Rosalind standing there, playing with the hem of her denim jacket and looking awkward. "You guys should probably up the security in here."

It's the first time she's coming to visit us.

Yeah, she's known all about us for some time now, but never seen us together in the flesh.

"You staying for dinner?" Julianna asks, beckoning her in.

"Um, sure," she says with a shrug. "I just wanted to let you both know that... I think you two are perfect for each other."

Julianna hands me the spatula and goes over and hugs her sister. "Thank you, Rosalind. That means a lot to me."

They share a smile.

The men pour in and sit down while she places all the food on the table. I know that they miss having this. My mom used to feed us all, but now that Dad has stepped down, she's been here less, enjoying a more private life at their own house. But with Julianna here, she's bringing that family vibe back to everyone.

Give a woman a clubhouse, and she makes it a home. That's how the saying goes, right? Or something like that anyway.

"Thank you for feeding us, Julianna," River calls out, and the men all mumble their thanks.

Small steps.

Julianna eats one taco and then kisses me on the cheek. "Me and Rosalind are heading home, I'll see you tonight."

"Bye, Julianna, love you!" Jeremiah calls out, grinning. His usual all-leather getup is a contrast against his almost white hair and light eyes, but Julianna tells me she likes his "BDSM" style. "And Rosalind, nice to meet you, sexy."

Rosalind rolls her eyes, but I don't miss the color in her cheeks.

"Love you too, Jeremiah," Julianna calls back, waving at everyone else. It's a weird arrangement with all of us, I have to admit, yet somehow I think it's going to work out.

When I see my grandma Cathy standing at the front of the clubhouse after dinner, I quickly go over to her. "What are you doing here?" I ask, frowning.

"I've come to say goodbye to you," she replies, expression guarded. "I'm leaving town to grieve my grandson."

"You have other grandsons here—you know that, right?" I say, even though I know the best thing is for her to go. There's no coming back from what she did, but that doesn't mean that it doesn't hurt.

"Victor was..." She trails off.

"Your favorite?" Yeah, it still hurts. I've known her my whole life. But I guess she isn't the person I thought she was.

"He didn't have anyone else. He had me."

There's a reason he didn't have anyone else. He was an asshole.

I cross my arms over my chest. "Where will you go?"

"You don't worry about that," she replies, her tone hardening. "I heard that Johnny and Libby are seeing each other. Let them both know they will get what's coming to them."

I watch her get into her car and drive off.

I did hear about Johnny and Libby.

Kind of weird, but also not surprised.

When people have something, you can just see it.

And they have something.

Just like Julianna and I do.

Epilogue

Julianna

One Year Later

I was always one of those girls who dreamed of her wedding day. I wanted the big wedding, the gown, the knight in shining armor.

I didn't picture rain, lots of rain.

And the ground turning into mud.

But I did get the knight on a motorcycle.

And my beautiful bridesmaids in their autumn colors, holding clear umbrellas, trying to save our hair and makeup.

The old me wanted the perfect wedding, but the grown-up me is just happy I got the perfect husband.

The one who cried when he saw me walking down toward him. Clad in all black, Johnny resembled a modern-day Johnny Cash.

The one whose eyes let me know that he thinks *he* is the lucky one.

So let it rain.

Let my curled hair get soggy, and my expensive heels sink into the mud.

It's the man next to me who brings my happiness, not other things that I can't control.

"Do you take this woman to be your wedded wife?"

"Well, I already did. But I do again," Romeo replies, emotion hitting him. "I so fucking do." Everyone laughs.

Smiling, I take him as my husband, and before we're told to kiss, Johnny whispers something in my ear. "My bounty is as boundless as the sea, My love as deep; the more I give to thee, The more I have, for both are infinite."

A quote from *Romeo & Juliet*, which couldn't be more appropriate for us.

The cheers come from the MCs. Our MCs now merged as one—Angels and Devils MC.

From our grandparents, who found each other again. Their love grudge now broken.

From our friends who loved us all along.

We united warring motorcycle clubs with our love.

And now the club is thriving. No one will step onto our territory with our numbers so strong, and our strength unyielding.

We walk back down the pathway hand in hand, ignoring the rain, still lost in each other.

He pulls me against him when we come to a stop, kissing me again. "I love you, Julianna."

"I love you, too," I reply, smiling.

"My bike used to be my happy place, my peace, but now that's you," he says with a smile.

He's so damn sweet. I kept my last name, and he doesn't mind. And any future children will carry both of our names.

Taking his hands, I place them on my stomach. "Are you ready to be a father?"

His eyes widen. I'd only just found out I was pregnant a few days ago, and I was going to wait until after the wedding to tell him, but I think everyone would notice if I didn't have a wine at my own wedding.

"Are you serious?" he asks, lifting me up in the air. "Just when I thought this day couldn't get any better!"

He kisses me again, and then we join the crowd, where the motorcycle club is all mixed up together. You wouldn't know who came from where, just like a blended family.

Sometimes you just have to follow your gut, and fight for what you want to get your own version of your happily-ever-after.

And I'm so damn happy that I did.

* * * * *

Acknowledgments

A big thank-you to Carina Press for working with me on this new series!

Thank you to Kimberly Brower, my amazing agent, for having my back in all things. We make a great team, always have and always will.

Brenda Travers—Thank you so much for all that you do to help me. I am so grateful. You go above and beyond and I appreciate you so much.

Tenielle—Baby sister, I don't know where I'd be without you. You are my rock. Thanks for all you do for me and the boys, we all adore you and appreciate you. I might be older, but you inspire me every day. When I grow up, I want to be like you.

Sasha—Baby sister, do you know one of the things that I love about you? You are you. You don't care what anyone else thinks, you stay true to yourself and I am so proud of you. Tahj reminds me of you in that way. Never change. I love you.

Christian—Thank you for always being there for me, and for accepting me just the way I am. Thank you for trying to understand me. We are so different, opposites in every way, but I think that's the balance that we both need. I always tell you how lucky you are to have me in your life, but the truth is I'm pretty damn lucky myself. I appreciate all you do for me and the boys. I love you.

Mum and Dad—Thank you for always being there for me and the boys no matter what. And thank you, Mum, for making reading such an important part of our childhood. I love you both!

Natty—My bestie soulmate, thank you for being you. For knowing me so well, and loving me anyway. I hope Mila sees this book one day and knows her Aunty Chanty loves her so much!

Ari—Thank you for still being there for me, ten years later. You are one of the best humans I've ever known.

To my three sons, I'm so proud of the men you are all becoming, and I love you all so very much. I hope that watching me work hard every day and following my dreams inspires you all to do the same. I love every second of being your mother. You will forever be my greatest blessings.

Chookie—No, I love you more.

Tahj—You make me so proud. You are silently protective of everyone around you. You are smart, and creative. I see you.

Ty—You'll be happy to know I've finished my "working shenanigans" deadline. Love you.

And to my readers, thank you for loving my words. I hope this book is no exception.

About the Author

New York Times, Amazon and *USA TODAY* bestselling author Chantal Fernando is thirty-six years old and lives in Western Australia.

Lover of all things romance, Chantal is the author of the bestselling books *Dragon's Lair*, *Maybe This Time* and many more.

When not reading, writing or daydreaming, she can be found enjoying life with her three sons and family.

For more information on books by Chantal Fernando, please visit her website at www.authorchantalfernando.com.